Praise for Radclyffe's Fiction

"...well-plotted...lovely romance...I couldn't turn the pages fast enough!" – Ann Bannon, author of *The Beebo Brinker Chronicles*

"...well-honed storytelling skills...solid prose and sure-handedness of the narrative..." – Elizabeth Flynn, *Lambda Book Report*

"...a thoughtful and thought-provoking tale...deftly handled in nuanced and textured prose that is both intelligent and deeply personal. The sex is exciting, the story is daring, the characters are well-developed and interesting – in short, Radclyffe has once again pulled together all the ingredients of a genuine page-turner..." – Cameron Abbott, author of *To the Edge* and *An Inexpressible State of Grace*

"With ample angst, realistic and exciting medical emergencies, winsome secondary characters, and a sprinkling of humor...a terrific romance....one of the best I have read in the last three years. Highly recommended." – Author Lori L. Lake, book reviewer for the *Independent Gay Writer*

"Radclyffe employs...a lean, trim, and tight writing style...rich with meticulously developed characterizations and realistic dialogue..." – Arlene Germain, *Lambda Book Report*

"...one writer who creates believably great characters that are just as strong as mainstream publishing's Kay Scarpetta or Kinsey Milhone...If you're looking for a great romance, read anything by Radclyffe." – Sherry Stinson, editor, *OutlookPress*

Change of Pace:

Erotic Interludes

By the Author

Change of Pace:

Erotic Interludes

by

RADCLY*f*fE

CHANGE OF PACE: EROTIC INTERLUDES

© 2004 BY RADCLYFFE. ALL RIGHTS RESERVED.

ISBN 13: 978-0-7394-6713-8
ISBN 10: 0-7394-6713-1

THIS TRADE PAPERBACK ORIGINAL IS PUBLISHED BY BOLD STROKES BOOKS, INC., PHILADELPHIA, PA, USA

CREDITS

EXECUTIVE EDITOR: STACIA SEAMAN

PRODUCTION DESIGN: STACIA SEAMAN

COVER PHOTO: RADCLYFFE

COVER DESIGN BY SHERI (GRAPHICARTIST2020@HOTMAIL.COM)

Author's Introduction

Erotica is one of those things that you know when you see. The dictionary loosely defines it as an art form designed to arouse. That was one intention when I wrote these selections, but I also find that erotica is a commanding medium for exploring the many nuances of lesbian sexuality. I try to infuse all my fiction with the power and grace of our physical language, but in writing erotica, I can focus the spotlight even more. The only "theme" of this first collection in the Erotic Interludes series from Bold Strokes Books is the fact that these are women in charge of their own sexuality, and enjoying it.

Thanks go to my editor, Stacia Seaman, for skillfully reviewing and assembling this collection; my beta readers Denise, Diane, Eva, JB, Jane, Jenny, Laney, Paula, Robyn, and Tomboy, for their always essential comments; and to HS and all the members of the Radlist for their enthusiastic support and unflagging belief in me.

I often tell Sheri she is a wizard when I send her a photo and she sends back a work of art. She always laughs when I say that, not realizing what magic she creates. I can't imagine a book of mine without her touch to hold it.

These days, more than ever, Lee keeps our life in order, my mind focused, and my heart free to dream. Partner does not come close to defining her place in my life. *Amo te.*

Radcly*f*fe, 2004

For Lee,

My Heart of Desire

TABLE OF CONTENTS

MIRROR IMAGES

Watching a woman come is the sexiest thing I've ever seen. There's such beauty in the emotion that pours uncensored from deep within to blush the skin with longing and need and, ultimately, joy. Hearing the broken cry of delight makes me clench inside and ache with wonder. Breathlessly viewing the tightening of fine muscles beneath delicate skin, the hitch of breath captured and then lost on a sob, the arch of neck at the moment of release pushes me to the very edge. Only the fear of missing one instant of her ecstasy keeps me from spiraling after her into that brief but exquisite *petite mort*.

The only thing I've ever found more exciting than making a woman come is watching her as she pleasures herself. A connection so intimate, so primal, lies beneath the hand that strokes her own flesh. Sacred communion, blessed rapture. Those are moments so wondrous, it hurts to watch.

It's a fantasy of mine, imagining what you feel as you stroke your need to a fever pitch, drawing the longing from your depths, coaxing the sweet song of passion to your clitoris, teasing yourself until there is no choice but to unleash the flood. Imagining what you feel as you grace me with the vision of your pleasure. I've always liked to think that you share the same fantasy. As I listen to the faint turn of metal on metal and watch the front door slowly open, I know that today, I'll find out.

You stop just inside, regarding me with pleased surprise. "Hey, love, you're home awfully early."

You kiss me swiftly on your way through the living room to the dining room to deposit your briefcase and shrug out of your blazer. Turning, jacket in hand, you regard me quizzically. I haven't moved. "What, hon?"

"There's something I want you to do for me."

You're not certain if it's something serious or if I want to play. What I love about you—*one* of the things I love—is that it doesn't matter. Your answer is always the same.

"Anything."

I extend a hand, and you take it trustingly. Your jacket falls abandoned by the wayside. I draw you to the bedroom, and for the first time, at the threshold, you hesitate. I've piled a nest of pillows in the center of the bed, but I can tell that's not what captures your attention. At the foot of the bed stands a tall mirror like the kind in clothing-store dressing rooms—sectioned so that it can be folded to give a complete view of the bed from several angles.

"Oh my." You sound a little breathless. Your eyes rise to mine, large and bright. "What—"

"Shh." I release your hand and step away, facing you as I reach for the buttons on my shirt. "Take off your clothes, baby."

As you begin to disrobe, so do I. Your nipples are already hard in anticipation. You *know* that before the afternoon is over, you will come. You don't know how, but just knowing that it will happen arouses you. My clit is stiff and throbbing. I have imagined this for so long. As I arranged the pillows hours ago, I was forced to stop and stroke my clit, the ache was so hard. I very nearly made myself come without intending to. I sat on the bed, doubled over, hovering on the brink of orgasm for minutes, my fingers clutching my clit. Now it pounds steadily from hours of being denied.

When we're both nude, I gesture to the bed. Wordlessly, we settle side by side, facing the mirror. The pillows piled high behind us allow us to sit nearly upright. I slide my left leg over your right, our only point of contact. Your thigh is tight, hot and trembling.

"Bend your other knee," I say gently. "You're so beautiful. Let me see all of you."

I hear your breath quicken, see desire glow on your skin as we open to each other, twin passions reflected in the glass.

"I want to watch you make yourself come," I murmur as I slowly draw the fingers of my right hand up the inside of my own thigh. My legs rest spread against the bed, as do yours, no secrets between us now.

"Oh yes." Your fingers brush softly, swiftly, over the smooth lips between your thighs. Moisture glistens there already, thick and heavy, dew on the rose. "Oh yes."

"Do just as I tell you."

Your hips lift when you hear my command, and your hand pauses in its tremulous quest.

"But I thought—"

Your voice holds a plea. *Already so ready, aren't you, my darling?*

"No matter what *I* do," I instruct as I draw a finger between my labia and smooth the thick come over my erect clitoris, "you may only do what I tell you."

I can see your eyes in the mirror watching my hands as I stroke myself. I know you can see the hard, red heart of my need. And knowing that you're watching makes my clitoris jerk beneath my fingers. I moan softly and draw my fingers away from the tip, knowing I will become far too excited if I am not careful.

Your fingers open and close, hovering about your own hard need. I know what you want to do. I can feel the pressure in my clitoris and know just how desperately you want to ease your ache. Unconsciously, your left hand has strayed to your breast, fingers squeezing a small, firm nipple. You fix on the mirror. Fix on the reflection of my fingers teasing the shaft of my erection. I allow you that touch on your breast. I want your pleasure, not your pain.

"Do you want to touch it, baby?"

You tug your nipple fitfully, your eyes glued to the mirror as I work my hard-on. "Ooh yes."

"One finger. And you can only stroke the top, on the hood. No more."

Instantly, your fingers fly to your clitoris, your hips jumping at the first touch. A small whimper escapes as you flick your fingers rapidly back and forth across the blood-thickened hood of your clitoris. Watching you, I forget myself and circle harder, stroking more firmly along the undersurface of my shaft. The ache grows huge. I want to come badly. Our hips rise in rhythm, four bodies moving in the shimmering fusion of reality and reflection.

"Touch the tip, very lightly." My voice is suddenly hoarse. Arousal presses heavily at my throat. "Make it wet, baby, make it shine for me."

I can hardly keep my voice steady. God, I want to get off. The muscles in my inner thighs are tight and my hips barely touch the bed. You are quick to obey, and I know how badly you ache for more contact, more pressure. Eyes hazy, you turn from the mirror to me.

"When can I come?"

"Soon, baby. Soon."

You look down at my fingers, wet with come. "Feels so good."

You or me? No difference now in our urgency.

"Stroke gently, but don't rub it. Do just as I say."

You moan again, the fingers of your other hand moving from your breast to your lower lips, parting them, easing inside even as you start the long strokes that will bring you off. Too soon. I want more; I want your soul.

"No. Not that yet."

Our legs twist on the sheet as we work our clits closer to coming. Abruptly, I gasp and tear my fingers from my clitoris. I felt the first warning spasms. I want desperately to come. I need so badly to explode. But I won't, because I won't let *you*. Not yet. I can see that you've begun to stroke yourself faster, without my permission, despite my instructions. Your eyes have partly closed, your lips have parted, and I know you want to come as badly as I. With my left hand, I reach between your thighs and touch your hand. Wetness seeps between your fingers as you rapidly circle the head of your clitoris.

I whisper the command. "Stop."

Body trembling, you obey. Your fingers press roughly against the base of your clitoris, unmoving. You begin to shake, and I know that the blood is rushing furiously into your length, making you hard to the point of pain.

Softly the words escape. "Please. Let me come for you. I need to come."

"I know you do, baby. I know." From beneath the pillows, I withdraw a cock and lean over, inserting it slowly between your lips, watching your eyes grow wide and your stomach tighten as you are filled.

"You're going to make me come," you whisper desperately. Your eyes in the mirror find mine as your lips part in silent supplication.

"No, I won't. I'll be careful." The base of the cock rests against your clit, your fingers plucking restlessly at the tip. "Don't move your fingers."

In the mirror, I watch the darkened head of your clitoris pulse, swollen and stiff, as it pokes from between your fingers. A single flick of a soft fingertip over the exposed head will bring you off instantly, shattering my soul. I twitch steadily, echoing your need. I am in danger of shooting my clit without even touching it.

My voice trembles. The cock pulses between your thighs. Your fingers are white as you hold your clit, hold back the orgasm you need so badly, holding on for me.

"Watch me. In the mirror." I withdraw another cock, settle it between my own engorged lips, and slowly draw the head up and down, gliding over my stiff clitoris, hips rocking gently with each thrust. The orgasm beats frantically in my belly, pounding to get out.

"I'm going to come soon," I murmur thickly, sliding the cock in one motion completely inside. The sudden stretch makes my clitoris lengthen and grow impossibly hard now. The extruded head rubs along the length of cock. I take my hand from yours and hold the cock deeply in place. In the mirror I see what you see, the dark red head of my clitoris as it throbs, resting against the shaft of the cock. I'm going to die if I don't come soon. With the fingers of my other hand, I grab the shaft of my clitoris and begin to rub the head back and forth across the smooth surface of the base of the cock. Immediately, my stomach clenches and the breath stops in my chest. Squeezing, I stroke the cock and my clitoris together, trying to watch in the mirror as the explosion gathers in the base of my clit.

I am groaning with each pulsation. Almost there.

You break. Hips thrusting in time with mine, the cock dancing between your legs.

"Please. Please," you cry, your fingers a blur on your clit, the other hand plunging the cock in and out between the lips that cling to it. "I have to come. I'm going to come. *Please* let me come."

I meet your eyes in the mirror and see my passion reflected. We are joined, cocks thrusting, fingers dancing, bodies poised on the point of explosion.

"Let me see you come, baby. Oh God, let me see."

Permission granted.

Crying out, you jerk upright, nearly sitting as the strong muscles in your stomach contract along with the inner muscles squeezing the cock.

You are coming, and when I see it, you make me come.

Dissolving beneath the flood of pleasure, I cling to your image in the glass, transfixed by all the beauty that is you.

CALL WAITING

It was supposed to have been a clear, warm May night, so I'd gone for the simple butch look with a black T-shirt and jeans and no jacket. It was the night I was certain I'd be spending the *whole* night with her, so I only needed to walk between the car and her house, and then her house and the restaurant around the corner, and then in the morning—well, who cared? I wanted to show off my arms a little, and you needed a T-shirt for that. What's a little chill when you're trying to look good for a woman.

We'd been dating for six weeks. Six weeks since I rounded a corner in the doctors' locker room, a toolbox in one hand and a two-foot length of metal edging in the other. Loose tiles in the ceiling needed replacing. I was wearing khaki work pants and scuffed work boots and a white T-shirt under my red cotton shirt. She wore a wisp of white lace over her breasts and a tiny triangle of pale blue between her thighs and there was a long, *long* expanse of toned, tan belly in between. Something gold glinted at her navel. I thought my heart would stop.

She stared at me, a surprised look in her eyes, and I said something really clever, like "Uh..."

Then her mahogany eyes wandered down my body, and I swear she checked out my crotch—but that couldn't have been right—my brain was just melting from trying *not* to look at her breasts. I felt myself blushing. *Blushing,* for Christ's sake.

"Uh..." I gritted my teeth. *I have got to do better than that.* "I'll come back."

"No," she said, smiling with just a little hint of laughter behind it. "Go ahead. Do what you have to do."

Then she turned to the locker and reached inside. The cracked piece of dusty acoustic tile was almost right above her head, and if I stepped up onto the wooden bench that ran the length of the aisle between the opposing rows of lockers, I could reach it. I sidled by her, being *very* careful not to even stir the air around her, which appeared to shimmer. It did, I swear to God. I put my toolbox on the floor and slid the inch-wide metal replacement strip through one of the loops on my sweat-stained leather work belt.

She was humming something low and throaty as she pulled out a blue scrub shirt. Flowers, I smelled flowers—her scent—something she'd dabbed on and something else uniquely her. My senses swirled with the heady mix while all the rest of the air was sucked out of the room. It was nine a.m. on Monday morning, and I was standing in the middle of the OR locker room in one of the busiest hospitals in the city. I had enough items on my punch list to keep me going until seven. But as the whisper of cotton brushed down her arms and over her breasts, I felt warm, sweet skin beneath my lips, felt the slow, hot burning start deep down inside, and forgot all about work. I shivered. I don't remember making a sound, but I must have, because she stopped, her scrub pants in her hands, and met my eyes.

"Need something?"

"I have to..." *Touch you, smell you, taste you.* "Climb up there behind you."

She angled her head, her dark hair trailing across one cheek, and studied the bench that came just to knee level. Her lips were deep rose, wide and full, and they parted just enough for me to catch a glimpse of the tip of her tongue. My stomach got tight, my clit twitched, and I got wet.

"Need help getting up there?" One arched eyebrow lifted.

Her sultry voice slid smoothly through my veins, hot as blood.

"No." *I'm already flying.* "I'll just be a minute."

She lifted one impossibly perfect leg and nudged a bare foot into the scrub pants. "Take your time."

I averted my gaze, because to look any longer would have risked spontaneous combustion, and besides, I wasn't sure she knew what she was doing to me. She could have just been a straight girl who didn't have a clue. I like looking, but only when invited. It only took me a minute to slide the damaged square of tile to one side, and I was just about to tap in the new piece of metal edging when she spoke.

"By the way..."

When I glanced down, arms still over my head balancing tools and tiles, I almost fell off the bench. I'm long in the leg and a bit taller than her, which in that position put her face right about even with my crotch. If I tilted my hips just a bit...

She raised her chin, gazing at me through long lashes. "Do you get a lunch break?"

I swallowed and forced myself not to move a muscle. I would *not* press my aching cli— "Uh-huh. Sure."

"Can I buy you a cup of coffee later?"

Not necessary. You already own me. I reached down deep for every inch of butch suaveness I could muster, which was just enough to hold back the whimper. "Right. Great."

Then she lifted a folded piece of paper in two fingers and ever so gently tucked it into the front pocket of my khakis. I almost came right there.

"My beeper number."

She drew away without touching me again, but I felt her hands on my hips, guiding me between her thighs.

"Call me," she murmured, and walked out.

"Yeah," I croaked through a throat thick with wanting. My watch said nine thirty. I'd never last.

But I lasted—until noon that day when we had coffee on the corner in front of the hospital, shoulders hunched against the late March wind. I lasted until the next time she wasn't on call, and we had dinner at a little hole-in-the-wall Mexican place around the corner from her apartment. I lasted through every date with her, when we'd talk about her work and mine and the news and the local sports teams and the state of the world. I lasted without touching her, except to kiss her good night, although sometimes the kisses lasted for hours. I lasted at least until I could get home.

Then I'd tumble into bed and think about her mouth while I slid my fingers up and down on either side of my clit. Her lips were so warm, so soft, when she brushed them over mine. It was so easy to imagine them licking me, sucking me, as I worked my swollen flesh between trembling fingers. I usually came fast, even though

I tried to wait, a swift hard come that ripped my breath away and left me moaning. It helped ease the ache, but it never assuaged the hunger. I'd wake up wanting her all over again.

But the worst was when she was on call. I'd see her around the hospital, but she wouldn't have any time for me. Mostly she'd be too hassled to do more than toss me a short, distracted smile. I knew she was busy, knew she couldn't get away, but it didn't stop me wishing we could sneak off for just a few minutes. Just long enough for me to rub my face against her neck, breathe in her smell, feel her thread her arms around my neck and give me one of those incredible all-over, pressed-tight-to-my-body, soul-deep kisses. Of course, the one time she *did* grab my arm, pull me into a stairwell, and shove me up against the wall to kiss me for a hot, heady minute, I had to go directly to the bathroom down the hall and make myself come the instant she disappeared. Leaning with my forehead against the cold metal stall, eyes squeezed tightly closed, jaws clamped shut against a groan, I shoved my hand through my fly, rubbed furiously for thirty seconds, and came in hot gushes all over my trembling fingers.

Oh, I lasted, all right.

But tonight was the night. I just knew it. Every time we'd been together, we'd gotten closer. Hell, the last time we'd been on the sofa in her living room, me with my hand under her blouse, teasing her nipple through another one of those lacy concoctions, her with her thigh pressed so hard between my legs, I knew she *had* to be able to feel my stiff clit, clothes or no clothes. We'd almost gotten there, and then she'd rolled away.

Stroking my face, she'd whispered, "You make me so hot. I could come just from kissing you."

"I think *I* might if you give me another minute," I'd gasped. *Jesus, let me make you come.*

But she'd just smiled. "Time for bed. I have to work tomorrow."

When I'd gotten to the door, she'd said, as she always did, "Call me."

I didn't even make it home that night. I drove three blocks, pulled the car to the curb in the shadow of a huge tree, and jerked off in the front seat—one hand braced against the wheel, my hips thrashing as I came with a hoarse shout. Then I sat there gasping for another five minutes until I finally managed to steady my hands and clear my head enough to drive.

So no one was more surprised than me when, after we had a great dinner at a small intimate restaurant, went back to her place, and ended up wrapped up in each other on the sofa again, it was *me* who put on the brakes. But while we were kissing and touching and starting to shed clothes, I felt something I'd never felt before.

I was on top of her, and she arched her back when I dragged my teeth down her neck. I looked at her—so exposed, felt her tremble—so vulnerable, and thought *I love you.*

She seemed a little confused when I eased back and just cradled her in my arms, stroking her hair and her neck and her back while we both panted unevenly and our hearts beat like crazy.

"I had a fantastic time," I finally murmured. "I'd better go."

Funny thing, she didn't say anything when I walked out the door this time.

Of course, the second I hit the street a little after midnight, lightning cleaved the sky, thunder roared, and a freezing rain beat down on my head like the world was coming to an end. The weather mirrored my mood. I didn't know why the hell I was leaving her, but I ran for the car and drove the twenty minutes home, all the while thinking, *So, I've never been in love before. Not this aching, can't breathe, gonna die if I can't have you kinda being in love. No reason to run. Big wimp.*

By the time I got home, I'd decided I was the biggest idiot in the world. A soaking-wet, shivering, and still very horny idiot. I walked though the apartment, grabbed a towel from the bathroom, and sat down on the side of the bed to rub the storm from my hair. The light on the answering machine was blinking, and I automatically reached out and pushed the play button.

The instant I heard her voice, I froze.

"Hi. It's me."

She sounded languid and warm, almost dreamy. My body tingled, and my heart leapt into my throat.

"I missed you as soon as you left. I keep feeling you—your hands, your mouth. I love the way you touch me."

The towel fell from my hand as I stared at the dusty brown plastic box on my bedside table. The blinking light said only one message. *PLEASE don't run out of tape.* I held my breath and prayed.

"I wanted to be yours tonight—I wanted you to have me—I wanted to give you some of the pleasure loving you gives me. Do you want me..."

Her breath caught and there was a second of silence. My hand shook as I pushed the volume all the way up.

"I imagine you here beside me now, watching me—watching me as I feel what you've done to me. Do you want to know how wet I am? How firm and hot and swollen? I'll stroke myself for you, let you watch me come...for you...only for you..."

Her soft moan cut straight through me. I wanted to crawl right through the phone line to get to her.

"I need you. Give me your hand—I'll show you. Yes—there... I'm so wet for you. Yes, touch me there...right there. Oh, God, I knew you'd know just how...yes, yes, please..."

I couldn't get any air. My head spun. I pressed my nails into my palms, hoping the pain would keep me from flying apart. She was whimpering out the words now between soft, uneven cries.

"Please...oh, just a little harder. Oh, I want you inside...deep inside...need to come..."

I groaned, wanted to weep. My heart was about to burst from my chest. She took a shaky breath, expelled it on a long, tremulous wail.

"You're making me come—oh, it's so good so good so goood..."

The tape scratched along silently for another few seconds while I shivered and shook, clutching the mattress to keep myself upright.

"Are you there? If you are, call me."

I heard a quiet laugh before the line went silent.

Nope, no way. I got up, walked back into the living room, and grabbed my car keys.

This was one message I was delivering in person.

FULL-SERVICE STATION

Have you ever had one of those days where the only thing on your mind was sex? Actually not even sex, precisely—just the physiologic response to the act. Scientifically speaking, the orgasm. Or more accurately, the need to have one. I was having one of those days. I awoke from a totally unsatisfying dream that had to do with some unidentifiable someone doing something indescribable to me that felt damn good but didn't quite go on long enough to get me the brass ring. What it *got* me was a restless, heavy feeling in the pit of my stomach and an ache between my legs that was exceptionally unpleasant. To make matters worse, my travel clock with its barely discernable numerals mocked me by announcing it was time for me to move my ass or be late for the site survey.

So I was both horny *and* cranky when I joined my opposite number for breakfast at what passed for a diner in some truck stop of a town in Missouri. I had just spent my second night in far less than four-star accommodations, and I had to negotiate with an upper-echelon henchman from a huge farming conglomerate for a piece of prairie on which to build a retirement community. I hated this part of the job. We wanted the land, this guy's company wanted to sell it, but we had to dance the dance. He'd point out the great view, I'd frown about prevailing winds and the difficulty with landscaping; he'd rhapsodize over the absence of air pollution, I'd point out the problem of no nearby major arterials and inaccessibility; he'd mention the river and the recreational possibilities, I'd fret about flooding and insurance rates. And we'd both smile a lot and say, "No, please, after *you*."

Things did not improve as the day progressed. It was blazing hot, and we must have traipsed through every cornfield within a fifty-mile radius of wherever the hell we were, and I was *still* horny. By dinnertime I was downright uncomfortable. My clitoris, I was convinced, had doubled in size since the morning. The waitress in the diner, a friendly gem of a woman about one year older than God, made my pulse trip. Hell, even inanimate objects such as trees and fireplugs were beginning to appeal. What I needed was a little time alone to do what I could to relieve the insistent pressure in my pelvis and the steady beat of blood in my clit. A self-induced climax wouldn't help for long—it usually didn't when I got like this—but it might at least keep the wildlife safe for another day.

Finally, out of acceptable alternatives, I returned to the Roach Motel. My sweatbox of a room hadn't improved since I left it. The bed was narrow, the mattress lumpy, and the shower cold. The motor court—an extremely generous term—offered no nightlife to speak of beyond the Axel Inn across the street. From the looks of the motorcycles out front and the size of the beer bellies on the guys hanging by the door, I didn't think I was going to find what I needed in there.

Forlorn, I stood by the grime-streaked window in the neon shadow of the flickering Budweiser sign and considered my options. As much as I wanted to satisfy my bodily cravings, I could not picture myself lying naked on that pathetic excuse for a bed and making myself come. I would truly feel depraved. The shower was out of the question—this dump did not come equipped with a removable, hand-held, adjustable-stream, pulsating-head, multispeed orgasm inducer (which some woefully uninformed people apparently use to bathe with as well). Besides that, there was something green growing in the corner of the narrow metal stall, and it was bigger tonight than it had been twelve hours ago.

I decided to go for a walk.

Once I was in the parking lot, it became apparent there was nowhere to go other than down Highway 66 and very probably into a rerun of *The Twilight Zone*. Although I was beginning to think that possibility looked pretty good when compared to the reality here, I headed toward the motel office instead—the only other room with a light on. Norman Bates was behind the desk.

"Do you have the local paper?" I asked.

"Sorry—used it for the dog to pee on."

Of course. I thought for a moment. "How about a listing for your local cinemas?" At least I could take my mind off my pelvis for a few hours, and maybe I'd be tired enough to sleep later. With any luck whoever had been working me into a frenzy the night before would be back to finish the job. The way my clitoris felt, I ought to make it into orbit well before I hit REM sleep.

"Movies? Ain't got but the one place—the Sexiplex over in Hooterville. Want directions?"

"Ah, no. Thanks." That would be perfect—me and the boys jerking off in the dark. I needed to go home, soon. "I'll just," I grabbed a xeroxed leaflet from a stack on the counter, "look this over!"

It advertised, of all things, professional massage. There must be a gimmick—how could a town without United Artists Theaters support a massage therapist? But the flyer looked authentic. It had all the right buzzwords—including holistic and mind/body attunement. Salvation!

I dialed the number from the flyer on my cell phone and was informed that they could take me in half an hour. Just enough time to shower (thank God I brought my sea feet or else I would have been showering in my heels) and drive there. Thirty minutes later I was standing in a ten-by-ten-foot, beige-on-beige waiting room talking to a Barbie look-alike. Uh-oh. But the corners were clean, there was no sign of entomological infestation, and I was having a very bad day.

So when she asked me, "Would you like the whole body treatment or just a partial?" I answered, "Give me everything."

She made a little note. "Man or woman?"

"It doesn't matter, as long as they have good hands."

She looked at me from under very thick, very dark lashes and smiled knowingly. She *was* kind of cute, now that I thought about it. Even her breasts, impossibly high and suspiciously round, looked suddenly inviting. Oh my god, my brain had finally surrendered to estrogen storm!

"An hour for the standard treatment, or..." she added in a husky tone, "ninety minutes for the special."

"I think I want it all," I muttered. She wasn't doing a thing to reduce the throbbing in my crotch.

She grinned and made another note. "Okay. Follow me."

She led me to a surprisingly nice cubicle—completely enclosed with muted recessed lighting and the requisite mood music playing in the background.

"Get completely undressed and lie facedown on the table. Sheets are there by the chair. I'll send in your therapist."

With that she was gone, so I did as she instructed. After I stripped, I climbed onto the massage table, drew the sheet up over my buttocks, and settled my face into the curve of the molded headrest. It was warm and quiet, and I began to drift. Distantly, I heard the door open, but I didn't register another presence until a hand glided lightly over my arm to the back of my head. I heard a body settle onto a stool in front of me, and then fingers insinuated themselves into my hair. I nearly groaned out loud, it felt so good.

"Before we start..." The fingers kneaded my scalp and a soft, throaty voice inquired, "is there anything you don't like, or something you'd especially desire tonight?"

It sounded like a man, but it could have been a woman impersonating Lauren Bacall. It didn't matter, because whoever it was was performing miracles on my scalp. The tension drained from my body as I rapidly went limp. "Um, no—whatever you usually do," I managed to mumble. God, it was nice to be touched. I thought I heard a faint laugh.

The masseuse moved to the side of the table and started working on my back, and that's when all my troubles began. Strong hands massaged the muscles along my spine, moving from my shoulders to the depression just above my buttocks, where they pressed and circled. It felt good, very good, *too* good. The rhythmic motion of probing fingers working out the chronic knots rocked my entire body against the surface of the table. The problem was, the only place it seemed to be affecting me was between my legs. The slow, steady manipulation was stimulating blood flow, all right, but most of it seemed to be pooling in my pelvis. I felt myself get wet. *Oh, Jesus. Bad timing.* My clitoris gave a little jump. *Oh! Very bad!* Circle, circle, press, press. *Ooh—yes, right there!* Pulse, pulse, twitch, twitch. *Time to start doing multiplication tables.*

Unfortunately, just as I managed to divert my attention from my crotch with thoughts of next week's corporate division meeting, the sheet was whisked away and resettled just below my buttocks. I felt a slight breeze across my bare ass, and the sudden exposure made me jerk. The thigh clench that accompanied it only tweaked my clit more. If that weren't bad enough, warm lotion was being spread over my cheeks, into the cleft between them, and slowly worked into my skin with long, smooth strokes. A bit of the heated oil dribbled down my ass and into the folds of my labia, mixing with my own hot come. I shifted my hips automatically, spreading my legs slightly. The oil reached the underside of my clit, warm as a tongue lapping at me. I bit my lip to hold back a moan. Mercifully, just when I was afraid I would start pumping my ass into the hands that worked my butt muscles, the touch stopped.

"Would you like it harder?"

Oh, fuck, yes. Harder, faster, deeper. "Fine," I choked. "Anything is fine."

I drew another shaky breath and squeezed my eyes tightly shut, determined not to disgrace myself in front of a stranger. But, oh God, I was on fire—my nipples were painfully erect, trapped against the cotton beneath me, and each time I shifted, a twinge of arousal beat a path straight into my clit. I was primed, had been all day—fuck, I was dying.

Ankles. That should be safe enough. I slowly relaxed again, soothed by the symmetrical sensation of fingers tracing up and down the muscles and tendons of both calves at once. I felt nearly bereft when the hands left me for a moment, only to gasp in surprise at their sudden return, warm and slippery with oil, sliding up the inside of my thighs. Automatically, I opened my legs further. The sheet was now a thin ribbon of material, transecting my body where my buttocks and thighs joined. Underneath the flimsy material, I knew that I was open and wet and ready. I held my breath as the fingers circled higher, working my inner thighs, certain they would stop any second. And then—oh God, a brush of skin over the tiny hairs surrounding my anus. It was as if there was a direct connection to my clitoris, because just that feather-light caress caused it to twitch.

I couldn't stop the reaction. My buttocks clenched, my pelvis lifted off the table, and my thighs separated. What I wanted—oh Jesus, what I *needed*—was to slip one hand under my belly and get my fingers on my clitoris. I knew that the barest of strokes across the tip, the lightest squeeze to the shaft, and I would explode. Oh God, I wanted to come. I grabbed the sides of the table and gritted my teeth. *Please, please, please—move away from there.*

I couldn't be feeling what I thought I was feeling. Because it felt a lot like a thumb, slowly pressing against the tight ring of muscle between my cheeks. *Mmm, so good.* I meant to say stop, but the muscles of my throat were paralyzed. I could only whimper faintly. *Oh, yes, yes, yes...*

Dimly, through the red haze of lust clouding my brain, I was aware of my pelvis pumping rapidly as I pushed back against the pressure slowly opening, then entering me.

"Oh God." This time I groaned aloud, didn't I?

As the digit penetrated the depths of my ass, the sensitive muscles slowly clenched around it. An answering spasm began in the base of my clitoris, extended into my pelvis, and twisted through my belly. This was going to make me come very soon. I tried to clear my mind, fight back the pleasure. The hand pumped my ass—once, twice—and my breath fled.

I needed to come so badly now—my head swam with urgency. My harsh breathing seemed to fill the room. "Please."

My voice a weak cry.

My ass rose and fell, pushing and pulling the thrusting digit in and out of the warm channel. Each time my hips descended, I pressed my pubis against the rough surface of the towels under my body, trying desperately to stimulate my clitoris enough to come. I wouldn't come, *couldn't* come, usually, without some contact at that most sensitive point. And I was so close already. *OhGodohGod. Just let me come. Just this once.*

Two fingers slipped through the thick come between my swollen lips, one sliding on either side of my clitoris. I whimpered, rapidly rolling my hips from side to side, needing just a little more pressure on the shaft to go over the edge. I heard low, frantic moaning, punctuated by small cries, and realized it was me. That was how I sounded when I was about to come. A fingertip slipped under the hood of my clitoris and stroked back and forth.

"Oh God, oh God, oh God—please, please, please." My head thrashed from side to side, my hips pounded, and the finger in my ass drove harder, faster. The orgasm built, unstoppable now. Nearly breathless, I teetered on the edge, every muscle painfully tense, mumbling desperately. "Gotta come now, please—gotta come, gotta come, oh—now, now, *now.*"

Fingers circled my clit, fingers fucked my ass, and then fingers claimed the last available orifice—I registered them filling me an instant before everything—head, belly, clit—exploded. Someone screamed; it must have been me. All I knew was the gripping spasms that started in my clitoris, rapidly flooded my pelvis, and flashed through my body, bursting into white lightning behind my eyes. I was groaning, pumping, gushing onto—well, it didn't really matter *whose* hand it was, did it? All that mattered was that *finally,* I was coming.

Whoever would have figured, in a town like that, such a full-service place as this?

RECONNECTING

By the time I finally got home, it was well after dark, and my clit was so stiff it hurt to walk. I'd been wanting her all day. Hell, I'd been wanting her for *days*. I'd been working late almost every night, and she'd been overscheduled every day. No time, coming or going. But it wasn't just the treadmill of day-to-day routine preventing us from connecting. Not just time, but something deeper, as if we both needed something from the other, but we couldn't—or wouldn't—say what. And when we couldn't read the message in the other's eyes, the silence left us both slightly forlorn.

To make matters worse, we'd had a fight. Well, not exactly a fight, more of a colossal misunderstanding. I had been selfish, and she had been disappointed. I hated myself for that—for being less than she had dreamed I would be—and I ended up feeling helpless. I'm very bad at feeling helpless. So I got withdrawn and edgy, and then she felt abandoned. The chasm grew. In the end, we both hurt far more than the initial affront ever warranted. Even though we'd eventually agreed that we couldn't get along without each other, we were still wary and uncertain. And even in bed, we were self-conscious about touching.

The longer we were estranged, the more apparent it became to me that she was everything I had ever wanted, and more. No one had ever matched me for intensity, or passion, or sheer devotion. I was beginning to think that I had not only met my match, but had been surpassed. She'd awakened desires I had long forgotten and inspired me to venture down paths I had only dared dream of.

Now, to be separated—severed—from the passion that had come to define my daily existence and shape my nightly dreams was more than unbearable. It was slow death.

Not being able to touch her was killing me. It wasn't just the sex I missed, but the connection that made me feel as if I had some purpose for being alive beyond mere existence. I was hers, and she was mine, and knowing that, life made sense. Without her, I was stumbling half-blind through a world of shadows.

Of course, I wasn't *thinking* of any of those things as I walked into the bedroom that night. She was already in bed, propped up against the pillows in an old, holey T-shirt, a faded, blue-striped sheet pulled up to her waist. I knew how she always slept, and she'd be naked under those thin cotton barriers.

"Hey, babe," I said.

She was reading something impossibly technical, the kind of thing she found relaxing. She tossed me a half-smile by way of greeting and went back to what she was doing. We were better, but we weren't quite there yet. We were moving around each other with that hesitant care that follows a fight. That small degree of separation is tolerable for most people, but not for those few of us who survive on the deeply intimate connection with one, and only one, woman. I was slowly dying of hunger.

Of course, I wasn't thinking of any of those things as I walked past her into the bathroom. What I was thinking was how damned hot she looked, all relaxed and warm and half naked. I was thinking that I hadn't had my hands on her breasts in days, or tasted her in what seemed like forever. What I was thinking was that I wanted her, every part of her, for myself. I wanted every breath she drew, every thought she contemplated, every beat of her heart to belong to me. If I hadn't almost lost her, I probably wouldn't have been so desperate to reclaim her.

Of course, I wasn't thinking any of those things as I strapped on the Dancer. What I was thinking was that my clit had been throbbing for hours, and I needed her fingers, her mouth, to bring me off. What I was thinking was that I wanted her to feel *me* in every part of her, deep inside, where there could be no doubt about how much I loved her or how much she loved me. What I was thinking was if she reached down and tugged on my cock just a few times, I would come. I wanted her to remember that she'd once said she adored me, that she belonged to me, that she was mine.

Of course, I wasn't thinking any of those things as I turned down the lights, crossed the room, and drew back the covers. She looked at me in surprise as I eased into bed beside her, leaning on one arm to look into her face. Then her eyes widened as she felt the length of my cock brush against her thigh. Her lips parted, a small sigh escaped, and the blue of her eyes became very dark. I usually don't come to her this way. I usually wait for her to let me know that she wants to be fucked. But that night I couldn't wait; that night my need was so great I could only think of taking her. I knew she would know what that silent admission cost me, and I didn't care.

"Do you need something?" she asked, her eyes never leaving mine as she reached down to fist my cock.

"Yes." My throat was dry. My stomach ached with the arousal that weighed heavy as a stone in my pelvis. I looked down, watched her curled fingers slowly tighten around the shaft, and I got wetter, harder.

"What?" she murmured, giving me a tug. "What do you need, huh, baby?"

The base pulled away from my body a fraction of an inch, then snapped back in the harness, striking my stiff clit.

I gasped.

"Is that what you need? You need to come in my hand?"

"In you," I whispered. "I need to come *in* you."

She smiled slowly. "Is that all?"

Then she tugged again...and again, faster and faster, beating me off until I choked out a cry and went rigid, ready to lose it right then, right there.

Then she stopped.

"What do you *want?*"

I could smell her desire. Her breasts rose and fell ever faster, the nipples small hard stones beneath soft cotton. I wanted my teeth on them, closing down until she cried out.

"I want to fuck you." My voice shook, and my arm trembled as I held myself above her. Waiting. Waiting for her to take me back.

"Why?"

"Because I need to feel alive."

She spread her legs and pulled me over her. I braced myself with a hand next to her shoulder, my knees between hers. Then she tilted her hips and let me settle my cock between her thighs. I wanted to weep.

"Why else?"

"I'm lonely." I put a hand between us, held my cock, and glided the head up and down between her legs, just barely touching her. "I'm empty—deep inside."

Smiling, her hips rolling with each stroke of cock through slick folds, she reached up to twist her fingers in my hair. She tugged my head down and caught my lower lip in her teeth, chewed on it as she pushed against the fat head, trying to take me inside.

Carefully, I stretched out on top of her, my breasts against hers, my mouth searching for her tongue. With my free hand, I guided the tip of my cock firmly between her labia, feeling the easy way it slid, knowing she was already wet. As my tongue danced with hers, I worked the head up and down between her lips, lightly pressing her clit, stopping just short of entering her. I palmed the cock and used it to tease her, all the while the motion rubbing my own rigid clit, edging me dangerously close to blowing. My whole body was trembling. I'd wanted to fuck her the minute I'd touched her. I almost didn't care if she was ready or not. I wanted her so badly, I had to force myself not to thrust into the places I needed to be. Her hands moved to my shoulders, digging into me so hard I could feel the imprint of her nails. She rocked herself up and down along the length of my cock and whispered in my ear, "Fuck me."

She always knows what I need. I felt like I might cry. I felt like I might raise my head and howl like a wolf calling for its mate, bathed in the silver light of the moon. I felt like an awestruck virgin, taking my first woman. I felt primitive, and powerful, and so goddamned grateful that she would have me.

I wanted to be inside her so much I was sick with urgency. I clenched my thighs and pressed the cock down against her. The head slipped in and she moaned, her spine bowing beneath me. My head went light and my heart beat an uneven staccato in my chest. I wasn't breathing. Shuddering, I sobbed for air.

"Come on, baby," she crooned, her fingers tugging my hair. "Come inside me."

I pushed again. The curve was perfect for us, and as she lifted her ass slightly off the bed, I slid it all the way in. She whimpered as I filled her, and I nearly came as the base rode up and down, rolling over the shaft of my clitoris. I braced myself with both arms then and started to stroke. My mind was a haze of red heat. I'd been so hard for her all day. She was all that was keeping me alive, and I wanted to feel every fiber of her. I wanted to touch every corner of her being. I wanted, I wanted, I wanted—

"Oh, fuck, I'm gonna come," I groaned.

"Not yet," she gasped, neck arched, her unfocused eyes struggling to hold mine. "Please, baby, wait."

Gritting my teeth, I pumped into her with all the strength of my need. Her hips were pistoning up and down my cock, driving me closer with every thrust.

"All the way," she moaned against my neck. "Fill me all the way, everywhere, when you come."

She locked her arms around my shoulders and her legs onto my back. Opening, she took me deep, took me home.

"I want you."

"Fuck me."

"I need you."

"Fuck me."

"I love you."

"Fuck me."

I closed my eyes, and I took all she offered. Thrusting wildly, as deep as I could, I started to come. I was clutching *her* now, whimpering, as the orgasm stole my breath and blinded me. All I could hear was her chanting desperately in my ear, "fuck me fuck me fuck me"

My hips kept working as my clitoris twitched and spasmed and my stomach contracted. I slipped one hand between us and, curling my fingers down into her wetness, felt her swollen clitoris squeezed against the shaft of the cock. I massaged it with my fingertips and she screamed. I compressed the base, got two fingers on either side of it, and stroked her. She convulsed and came all over the cock, came for me and no one else.

"don't stop, don't stop, don't ever stop"

"never, never, never"

RUNWAY BLUES

I woke to the sound of the sea, the gentle swaying of the bed, and a soft moan.

Swaying bed? Soft moan? What the hell?

The night outside the adjacent window, which was cracked open an inch to allow a whiff of cool salt air to float in, was still dense with fog. I was lying on my back in an unfamiliar room in a bed I didn't recognize. Even more disconcerting was the fact that a near stranger was lying next to me, and I was pretty certain she was masturbating.

I should probably start at the beginning, which was approximately twelve hours ago. I arrived at the airport in Philadelphia the requisite two hours before my scheduled flight to Boston. I've never liked to fly, and ever since the new security regulations were instituted, I like it even less. I should've known that it was going to be one of those trips when I pulled into the economy parking lot, which is about the size of a small state, and saw the signs saying Lot Full. I prepared myself for even more inconvenience but was pleasantly surprised when I was given an economy-rate voucher to park in the short-term parking garage adjoining the terminal. Amazing. A savings of both time *and* money.

I made the mistake of taking this as a good omen.

It was Friday of the long Fourth of July weekend, and I hadn't been able to leave the lab any earlier. I'd been waiting for a protein sample to make its way through the filtration column, and that's a process that just can't be rushed. Still, I'd arrive in

Provincetown in the early evening and be able to enjoy a good start on the weekend. The line for the US Airways ticket counter wound its way through the path mapped out by steel poles and black nylon straps and overflowed into the main thoroughfare. I, however, had my Visa Preferred card, which even though I was traveling coach allowed me to check in at first class, where there were only two people waiting. I was checked in, had my boarding pass, and made it through security in forty-five minutes. Right on schedule for my 4:30 flight.

Two minutes before boarding, the US Airways agent at the gate announced that all flights into Boston were being delayed because of severe weather—there'd been intermittent thunderstorms throughout the Northeast for the last two days. I settled back into my seat in the crowded waiting area, glad that I had scheduled over an hour between my arrival in Boston and the departure on Cape Air to Provincetown. Unfortunately, my flight was an hour late leaving Philadelphia, and by the time the airspace over Boston was cleared from the earlier delays, I had missed my connecting flight. The agent at the Cape Air counter couldn't have been nicer.

"Hi there," he said with a smile.

I tried not to snarl. "I just missed my flight to Provincetown."

"Well," he said jauntily, his smile still in place, "the next scheduled flight is in an hour and it's full, but I *think*..." His fingers danced on the keyboard and he made little humming sounds that made me want to choke him, "they're adding another plane on that route because of the backlog. Hmm. Yes. Here it is." He looked up, proud of himself. "I got you on that flight."

"Thanks," I said, embarrassed by my earlier surliness. I took my new boarding card and hurried toward yet another security checkpoint. My luggage had been checked through from Philadelphia to Provincetown, and I only had a small carry-on with my computer and the newest Jessica Casavant. The tiny waiting area at Gate 33, the only gate servicing all of Cape Cod, was chaos. The last three flights to Martha's Vineyard and Nantucket had been canceled because of fog over the cape. The earlier storms had drifted off the mainland and now shrouded the ninety-mile, narrow finger of sand that was the vacation destination of tens of thousands of people this weekend. And it looked as if all of us were stranded in Boston.

Feeling secretly grateful and a tiny bit superior, I worked my way through the crowd to the check-in counter for Provincetown, the last hurdle before I could complete my journey. I'd be in town by ten thirty, with plenty of night left still. As soon as I deposited my luggage at the Provincetown Inn, I was going to head out to the Pied, one of the hot dance spots for women. Stress always makes me horny. And it had been a *very* stressful evening.

I passed my boarding ticket across the counter triumphantly. The young woman on the other side looked up sympathetically. Uh-oh.

"Hi," she said with a slightly less brilliant smile than the previous agent. "We just heard that the last two flights to Provincetown were diverted because of fog. We're canceling the rest of tonight's flights."

I heard a mournful groan and turned to see a blond about my age with a backpack slung over her shoulder and a frantic expression in her eyes.

"Sucks, huh?" I muttered. "You headed to Provincetown?"

"Yes, and I'm beginning to think I'm cursed. I've been trying to get three hundred miles for what feels like three days. God, I just should've driven."

"Me too. I would've been there by now." I laughed and held out my hand and told her my name.

"Kiera Jones." She closed long, warm fingers around mine. Her hand, I noticed, was strong and very soft. A musician's hands, or at least what I imagined a musician's hands would feel like. I probably thought of that because a guitar case leaned against her blue jean–clad leg.

"Vacation?" I asked.

She shook her head. "No, a weekend gig at the Crown and Anchor."

I knew the place in the center of town. It was best known for its drag shows and men's bars, but there was also a small lounge in the front. "Playing tonight?"

"No, thank God, or I'd really be crazy. Tomorrow and Sunday."

I turned back to the ticket agent. "Can I get on the first flight tomorrow?"

"I've got three hundred passengers from the other canceled flights to reroute. I *might* be able to get you on a flight late tomorrow afternoon."

"Thanks, but forget it. I'll rent a car and drive."

A man standing next to me at the Nantucket counter snorted. "Good luck. They've been canceling flights out of here all day. The last I heard, all the rental agencies were out of cars."

I glanced at the clock. Nine forty. The last ferry had already left for Provincetown. That left buses or limo services. I didn't care if I had to walk, I wasn't spending the night in Boston.

"I have to get to Provincetown tonight," Kiera muttered from behind me. "I've got sound checks and a run-through of the set first thing in the morning, and I've never played with these guys before. If I don't show up, they're going to think I blew them off."

I turned. "I'm going to see if I can get a private car. You want to share the cost?"

Her eyes lit up fleetingly, but then she shook her head. "Thanks, but—"

"Look," I said. "I'm going to do it anyway. Why don't you come along and just handle the tip."

"That's not fair."

"If you don't come, I'll be out the cost of the tip. Besides, I'd like the company."

She gave me an appraising glance, and it wasn't hard to figure out why. It sounded like a come-on, and I suppose on some level, it was. She was easy on the eyes, with shoulder-length, sun-kissed hair, luminous green eyes, and a wide expressive mouth. Beneath a short Levi's jacket, she wore one of those tight white tops with the thin straps that look like you should be sleeping in it and not wearing it outside on the streets. It barely reached the top of her low-rider jeans, and a small strip of tanned skin showed between the two. That narrow band of smooth belly begged for a touch, or at least that was the opinion held by all eight of my fingers.

"No strings," I said, too quietly for anyone else to hear. She had to know from looking at me in the Dockers and polo shirt I'd worn to work where my interests lay. Stereotypes come from somewhere, and I knew that my short dark hair and rangy build, along with my debonair style, spelled dyke. "Just a little friendly companionship."

"We can start there." She grinned and hefted her guitar case. "Let's go to P-town."

It wasn't all that difficult to find a limo. The airport was crawling with drivers hawking private rides to just about anywhere at exorbitant prices. The trick was finding someone who looked reputable who wasn't going to charge me my entire budget for the weekend. I could afford to rent a limo, but I couldn't afford to *buy* one. We finally connected with someone who fit the bill, and as we followed him outside into the steamy, overcast night, juggling our bags, I glanced at Kiera. "Things are looking up."

"Things are definitely looking up," she noted with a tilt of her chin.

I followed the direction of her gaze and whistled. "He didn't say it was a stretch limo. Well. Let's ride in style." I put down my luggage and beat the driver to the rear door, opened it, and gestured to the interior. "Ms. Jones. If you please."

She laughed in a wholly unself-conscious way, making her appear even more youthful than she was. *I'd* said no strings, but I hadn't anticipated the little zing that my *heart*strings gave at that moment. I climbed in after her and looked around. Wide leather seats, a minibar, and an honest-to-God live rose in a small glass vase tucked into a recessed niche in the door. Even better was the opaque Plexiglas that completely separated the driver's compartment from ours. I'd been in one of these limos before, and I knew that he could not, in fact, see us. Suddenly, as I settled next to Kiera, that seemed very important.

"This is wild," she said, leaning forward to examine the contents of the minibar. She cast me a mischievous look over her shoulder. "Do think we can drink any of this?"

"Why not?"

She settled back with a bottle of fairly good champagne in her lap. "Now what?"

I opened a small compartment next to the minibar and took out two glasses while Kiera popped the cork. As we headed out of Boston, we touched glasses and sipped champagne. I was definitely looking forward to the two-and-a-half-hour trip. We finished off the champagne at a leisurely pace and talked a little bit about the things that people do when they first meet. Then, on impulse, I asked, "Would you play something for me?"

Once again, Kiera regarded me with a mixture of curiosity and caution. Whatever she was looking to find, or *not* find, must've been there. Wordlessly she nodded and opened her guitar case. I said nothing. There were times when the only answers came from listening, not asking.

I watched her hands as they moved on the strings. I've always been fascinated by hands that create. Music, art, passion. Hers made much more than music, they made promises—or so I wished. But I contented myself with the beauty that filled the air. Sad, poignant notes, rich with stories of love and loss.

"You play the blues."

She looked up, her eyes dark and deep. "Surprised?"

"You hide it well."

"Everywhere but here," she observed, glancing down at her guitar.

"Beautiful." And I meant more than the music.

She must've known, because she carefully set the guitar aside and edged closer on the seat. I sat perfectly still and let her choose the song. She slid under the arm I had placed along the back of the seat and turned against my side, her arm coming around my waist. I dipped my chin so she could have my mouth if that was her desire, and she explored my lips with the moist tip of her tongue and the soft brush of her lips. Her breasts pressed against mine, her nipples hard. I slid my hand up to rest my cupped fingers just below the swell of her breasts. If she wanted me to touch her there, she had only to shift the slightest bit into my palm. She didn't, and I contented myself with what she offered. Her kisses were a feast unto themselves, long and languid and hot. She nibbled my lips, sucked my tongue, and teased the inside of my mouth with possessive strokes. She kissed me until I was dizzy and then some. At some point I felt her leg curl onto my thigh, and I felt the heat of her center where she pressed ever so gently against me in time to the thrusts of her tongue. I was going to soak right through my pants I was so turned on, and she still hadn't moved her hand from my waist. I groaned softly, imagining I would die if her hand found my skin, or if it *didn't,* and heard her laugh.

"Excuse me," a mechanical voice said from a speaker behind us.

I groaned again, long and low, as Kiera moved away.

"Yes," I said hoarsely.

"I can't see."

"*What?*"

"The fog is so thick I can't see the road. I'm gonna have to stop soon."

"Jesus," I muttered, trying to get my brain to function as Kiera repacked her guitar. "Where are we?"

"I haven't made very good time," Mr. Mechano said. "Somewhere on the cape."

"What do you suggest?"

Silence.

I blew out a breath as I felt the car slow to a halt. I looked at Kiera. "We'll have to get a room and wait this out."

"On the Friday of Fourth of July weekend? Good luck finding a vacancy." She smiled ruefully and traced a finger along my jaw. "But I guess we've been lucky so far."

I nodded and spoke to the voice. "Hello?"

"Yeah?"

"Go ahead and find us someplace to stay. Will you take us the rest of the way in the morning?"

"I'll sleep in the car. As soon as it clears, we'll go."

"Okay."

The limo moved on and miraculously, the driver did find us a place. We were too far from the bigger tourist attractions for the myriad of little motels dotting the cape to be full. Which is how I came to be in bed with Kiera. When we got to the room, whatever confluence of heart and harmony brought us together in the limo had drifted away on the fog. I could tell by the efficient way she went about stowing her gear and avoiding my eyes.

"What now?" I asked, unable to hide my regret and being unable to think of anything else to say that wouldn't sound ridiculous after what we'd just been doing.

"I'm beat," she said quietly, meeting my gaze. "I've been on the road since five this morning."

I nodded, standing on the far side of the bed.

"And," she added, "I don't usually have sex with strangers."

"Kissing isn't sex," I pointed out.

"No, it isn't. Technically." She glanced at the bed. "But this would be."

"I can sleep..." I glanced around. No sofa. There wasn't even a bathtub. "Really far away."

Kiera laughed. "Let's just go to sleep."

We stripped down, or at least I did. I didn't look in her direction. There was no way I was going to be able to sleep, not with the way my body felt after the crazy day and the miraculous kisses.

I crawled under the stiff cotton sheets, murmured, "Night, Kiera," and closed my eyes. The next thing I knew I was awake again, and so, it seemed, was Kiera.

I had no idea the time, or how long I'd been asleep. It might have been three hours or thirty seconds. Her breathing was shallow and fast, and I sensed, rather than felt, the sheet gently brush over my arm where it lay across my stomach as hers stroked rhythmically between her legs. She moaned again, very quietly, and I felt her leg tremble against mine. I didn't even stop to consider proper etiquette in this situation.

"Kiera, I'm awake," I whispered.

"I couldn't sleep." Her voice was thick and breathy. "Your kisses kept me awake. And I really need...to sleep."

"I can go for a walk," I offered, since standing in the shower with the water running seemed stupid. "Or you can just finish now." My own breathing had gotten a little short and my stomach was in knots. I hadn't been sleeping long enough for the blood that had pooled in my pelvis to move out. I was still hard. Knowing that she was too only made me more so. "I'd...like that."

She turned on her side to face me, her eyes a mere glimmer in the dark room. "Would you kiss me again while I do?"

I answered with my mouth on hers, and her tongue instantly filled me. Her leg came over my thigh again, this time with skin on skin, and she moaned softly. As I bit her bottom lip and tugged it with my teeth, I felt the back of her arm slide down my abdomen in the sliver of space between us and I knew where her hand had gone. Her body jerked, my head got light, and I realized I'd stopped breathing. I didn't want any sound to compete with her song now. I touched her bare breast very lightly and she arched, pushing into my hand. I rolled her nipple under my thumb, and she rocked against me. I could tell from her frenzied kisses and the rapid, rolling motion of her arm that she was getting close. My ears began to buzz, and I was afraid I'd pass out from holding my breath, but her staccato cries tore through me like sweet daggers, and I didn't want to miss a single note. I squeezed her nipple, hard.

Back bowing, she tore her mouth away and screamed, "Oh, God!"

"Oh, yes," I murmured, straining to see her face. She trembled and kept touching herself, keening softly, and I wanted to weep from the beauty of it. At last she lay quiet and spent in my arms while my heart thundered and my blood raced.

"You make such beautiful music," I whispered, stroking her face. I kissed her forehead, and she laughed quietly.

"I don't usually perform that one in public."

"I'm honored." I shivered, so aroused I was nearly sick with need.

She pressed closer and I felt fingers circle over my belly.

"Kiera," I whispered. "What—"

"Time for the encore," she murmured just before the applause began.

THE WOMAN IN THE SHADOWS

She was there in the shadows—my virgin lover, my longtime friend. I thought I would be more self-conscious, allowing her to witness what I had before only let her glimpse through my words to her, to others. She knew me, the best of me— my secrets, my dreams, my desires—because I had given her my passion cloaked beneath the veil of my musings. I had given her my poetry, my prose, my stories. She knew me, but never in the irrevocable, immutable way she would know me after the moments to come—never through my actions, through the inarticulate voice and stumbling phrases of my inadequate body. So much less eloquent, so much less beautiful, so much less—me.

I never asked why, in all the years of our companionship, she had never reached for me, nor I for her. Now I wondered only briefly what of me she would see that I had never meant for her to view, and what price those revelations might exact. I risked that she would turn from me, but I would not turn back. I could not lose what I had never had, and love without knowing is never love at all.

Amsterdam—a business trip, a book signing, a late-night stroll into the infamous red-light district. Narrow streets, tall crowded houses fronting uneven sidewalks, women behind glass, beckoning with gentle hands and secret smiles. There was a story behind every smile, and behind every window a bit of truth, if we dared to look. I tried not to, but as we walked, bare-breasted women posed within touching distance, warm and welcoming beyond the invisible barriers that might be breached for as little as the price of my latest book.

After the third time I'd glanced for longer than a fleeting moment, too long to be casual interest, my companion asked, "Do they attract you?"

I hesitated. She had never asked, and I had never told. "Yes."

"Why? They're strangers." She tilted her head, regarded me with soft curiosity. "Or is it only their bodies you desire?"

"Yes," I uttered, then quickly, "no." I sighed and met her kind eyes. "I think...they know me, what I need."

"What you need from a woman?"

Her voice was so soft, so gentle, and I feared I would hurt her, sooner rather than later. Knew without a doubt that she could hurt me.

"No." Afraid to touch her, I put my hands into my pockets. "What I need to give."

"And what is that?"

I shrugged, grimaced helplessly. The wordsmith struck dumb. "You've read it, countless times."

"Yes, I've read it." Her fingers were a whisper on my skin as she stroked my arm. "But I haven't *seen*."

We'd stopped in the middle of the sidewalk beneath a large tree in full leaf that shattered the pale yellow glow from a streetlight at the end of the block and painted fractured patterns on our faces. Three feet away a woman watched from a pool of shadow in an arched doorway. I could not see her face, but I could smell her perfume. Sweet as a summer night. I ached for the distance between us all as we stood so close, strangers in an intimate ménage.

"What do you want?" I murmured to my friend, to the woman in the door, to myself.

"To have nothing between us," my friend replied.

"Anything *you* want," the woman crooned.

To feel, I thought. *To give.*

"Together?" I asked uncertainly, afraid I had misunderstood. Afraid that I had not.

"No," my friend replied, shaking her head as if I were slightly slow, but unwittingly endearing. "I want to *see*."

The word hung in the air, a thundercloud of challenge and change.

"Just a minute."

As I followed the woman through the doorway and up the narrow stairs, I almost forgot that this was not a dream, not a fiction I had spun. The room she led me to was less tawdry than I had expected, small and surprisingly warm. A single bed—a clean white sheet turned back like the flap of an envelope waiting to be filled, a single lamp—its rose-colored shade tinting the muted glow with innocence, and a single chair—deep-seated and broad, pushed back to the edge of the room beyond the circle of illumination. The street noises, fragments of laughter and rumbling engines, floated in through the open window, reminding me that this was real. She stopped by the side of the bed and waited, allowing me to observe her. Far braver than I, for though we were strangers, we would touch more than flesh.

She was lovely actually, my aesthetic eye told me—beyond young but full bodied and well proportioned, her eyes clear and her gaze calm. As she slipped out of her blouse and slid the sheer material of her thigh-hugging skirt down her legs, she did not look to the shadows behind me where my friend sat in the deep easy chair. She looked at me.

She watched me watch her, and when she smiled softly at the appreciation in my eyes, I knew it was going to be all right. She must have recognized my astonishment, my wonder, my longing, for her expression became tender, saying wordlessly that she understood.

"Do you want to help?"

Her voice was throaty and full.

"Not yet," I murmured. "I want to look at you."

She wore a crimson thong and a scant froth of lace across her breasts that could only imaginatively have been called a bra. It barely covered her nipples, and the round, hard thrust of them against the whisper of silk brought desire twisting into my throat. Her breasts were average only in their size—naturally high and round and begging to be released from the fragile constraint of cloth. My hands trembled, eager to reach out, to gather the soft weight of them in my palms. I was still fully clothed, in a white cotton shirt and blue jeans. I wasn't wearing anything underneath, and the slight space between my flesh and the denim grew smaller, tighter, as heat and need made me swell and throb. She was beautiful in the way women can be when they smile at you, full of secrets and the promise to reveal them all for the simple price of a perfect touch. I wanted her like an ache in my bones, not to take, not to possess, but to worship.

"I know what you want," she whispered.

I watched her breasts rise and fall, more quickly with each passing moment. A faint flush deepened to rose on the creamy skin of her throat. The need in my belly opened and closed like a fist, and I moaned quietly.

So softly only I could hear, she beckoned. "Give me your desire. I am not afraid."

As I moved close to her, I no longer heard the voices from below, or the occasional blare of horns, or the quiet steady breathing of my friend. What had begun as a gift to one had become homage to another. In the dim light and dancing shadows, there was only this woman waiting for my touch.

I reached behind her with trembling hands, her nipples just grazing my chest, and slipped the clasp on her bra. As it came away in my hands, I brought my lips to hers, tracing the gentle arch and warm, firm curves with my tongue. She grew still, seemingly surprised at the kiss, and only after I persisted, gently pushing past the reluctant barrier into the oasis of her mouth, did her tongue hesitantly touch mine. As our tongues tumbled and twined together, I cupped her breasts in both hands, brushing my thumbs over her nipples, curling my fingers around the sides, squeezing gently. I pressed them together until they rose, firm and white, and I was forced to bury my face between them. My teeth scraped skin and her hips pressed forward against my pelvis. I eased away and found her lips again, brushing mine over hers as I thumbed her nipples faster.

She murmured something against my mouth in a language I didn't understand as she reached for the buttons on my shirt. I hadn't expected that either, but I let her expose me. She peeled the fabric down my arms; I released her breasts long enough to shrug the shirt off, then caught in my fingers the thin triangle of silk that slashed across her thighs. While she smoothed her hand through the hair at the back of my neck, I leaned down to guide the thong along her thighs, over her calves, and away.

With my face close to her gently rounded belly, I caught the scent of her arousal—rich and thick and heady. So I was not alone in my need. My own desire pulsed like a living thing from my depths, soaking my jeans, slicking my ready flesh.

"You're beautiful," I murmured.

She laughed and squeezed the back of my neck, then rapidly turned her palms to my chest and swept her fingers once across my bare nipples. The movement caught me by surprise and I gasped, lifting my breasts to her touch, but her hands were already gone.

"Are you sure you don't want me to touch you?" she asked, her fingers in my hair again. "I know how wet, how hard, how aching..."

"Yes," I choked, rising to press my denim-covered thighs to hers. Our breasts met as arms encircled backs, pelvis met pelvis, and lips strayed over sweat-moistened skin. My legs trembled. I heard the air pass harshly from my lungs. "I'm all of that," I murmured with my mouth to her ear, "from needing you."

"I'm here."

As we stood alone in the still circle of our desire, I had no awareness but the urgent need for her pleasure. I slipped my hand between our bodies, skimmed down her belly and between her thighs, and clasped her softly. With a short, deep sigh, she moved against my palm, anointing me with her essence. With a single finger, I parted her, scarcely breathing myself, and stroked slowly between swollen lips, ending at the full prominence of her clitoris. When I caressed her there, she gave a small cry and jerked slightly in my embrace. The exhilaration pierced me so strongly I thought I might fall, and I moaned a prayer of thanks.

"Is that good?" I questioned softly, two fingers caressing her length. She was very hard and so fragile.

"Too good, unless you mean for me to come now."

When she leaned heavily against me, shaking, I stilled my fingers and guided her backward to the bed. "No. Not so soon."

She sank down gratefully and rested back on her arms, facing me as I stood between her parted thighs. "But not too long, please."

As I knelt to complete my adorations, I wondered fleetingly what image my friend saw as she looked at us. Did she witness the supplicant at the shrine? Did she sense my awe, my gratitude? If I did not think she could, I would never have come this far with her. She had asked to see beyond the surface of my pages to the heart of my story, and now she would. I could not stop now, not with my body set to bleed.

The scent of welcome captured me then, and I thought of the one in the shadows no longer. Warm and rich, like fertile earth, this woman's arousal called to me—drawing me down as if hypnotized. One hand above, exposing her, one below, entering her, I opened her to my devotions. I drank the evidence of her desire, astonished anew at the sweet heady taste. Her need beat against my lips like a desperate caged bird, and I didn't have the strength to resist any longer. I took her quivering clitoris into my mouth, first sucking gently, then pulling her deeper so that my tongue could tease the turgid shaft, working it rhythmically from side to side, then circling to ease the pleasure so much like pain.

Her muted cries shivered along my spine, and as I held her tightly in my mouth, I fumbled open the buttons on my jeans. Senses reeling, I touched myself, stroked her. Gasping, feeling the answering surge of her hips, I worked myself harder, careening toward orgasm. I felt what she felt—the burgeoning pressure inside as muscles contracted around thrusting fingers, nerve endings dancing as exquisitely sensitive flesh readied to explode. I heard nothing, saw nothing, knew nothing—nothing but my mouth on her and my fingers squeezing, pulling, tug—

She cried out, and that sweet sound stilled my hand as only her pleasure could. This was for her. When she pressed upward against my face, I sucked once, hard, and I felt her spasm between my lips. I shuddered as she came, a stroke away from joining her. I closed my eyes tightly, waiting, until she began to quiet, and then I gently brushed my fingertips over my tense clitoris. The orgasm broke over me and carried me helplessly away. If we were not alone in that moment, I never knew it.

How much later I stirred, I do not know. I eased my fingers from inside her, and she moaned a soft protest. I stood, lifted her legs onto the bed, and pulled the sheet over her. I brushed away a stray lock of hair caught in the corner of her mouth, and she rewarded me with a kiss against my palm before closing her eyes with a long sigh.

I turned from her, my legs still shaking, and buttoned my jeans. A hand extended from the dark, offering my shirt. I took the shirt in one hand and reached for my companion's with the other. We would walk for a while. The night was not over, and there were other stories to tell.

HART'S DESIRE

Rian Hart slammed the desk drawer and sent a tremor rippling across the floor, up the metal rungs of the associate editor's chair, and into his ass with enough force to nearly knock him over as he leaned back, contemplating the pattern on the acoustic ceiling tiles.

"Something wrong?" he asked cautiously, lowering his shoes from atop his blotter and tipping forward until his elbows met his desk.

"No," she snapped, pushing aside a stack of files so violently that several caromed off onto the floor. She ignored them, hunched her shoulders, and pounded her keyboard relentlessly. "Deadline."

"Plenty of time yet." He tapped a pencil aimlessly, producing an annoyingly unsyncopated patter. "Doing anything special tonight?"

"No," she answered again, quietly this time. She didn't look at him. She tried to ignore her disappointment. *It's not like Valentine's Day really means anything, for heaven's sake. It's just another excuse for commercial exploitation. So she forgot. It doesn't mean she doesn't love me.*

She stared at her monitor, the words a blur. *Does it?*

A tiny sliver of uncertainty pricked at her consciousness. She *had* been out of town a lot lately, traipsing back and forth across the country following yet another missing-wife case. They hadn't had much time alone—or much time for much of anything when they *were* together. There had been that quick visit she had made

43

to the hospital between a morning flight in from California and an evening flight out to New York City at the beginning of last week. She smiled at the memory. She did enjoy their grappling like teenagers in heat on the narrow bed in Bren's on-call room. But it was hardly the height of romance. Had it really been almost two weeks since that brief flash of intimacy?

A surgeon and an investigative reporter—whatever had made them think they could keep a relationship afloat? But they had. So far. So she thought.

Maybe they were losing the romance. They were well past the honeymoon period. They didn't live together but they slept together every night—well, except on those nights when Bren was on call or Rian was chasing a story. Such day-to-day intimacy could dull the excitement. Was Bren getting bored with her?

Rian sighed, crammed her notes into her briefcase, and snapped it shut. She glanced at the clock. It was after six p.m. already. "I don't think we'll be doing anything. Bren hasn't called. She's probably still in the OR."

"Maybe she tried sending flowers and the guy couldn't find the office."

"Yeah. Right." But she smiled faintly as she gathered her things and headed for the door. "Night."

The hall was empty and most of the adjoining offices were dark. Her footsteps echoed eerily down the long, dim corridor. She'd just reached the sidewalk in front of the Tribune building when a man stepped forward and inquired politely, "Ms. Hart?"

Rian stopped, instantly alert, but not particularly worried. Medium height, middle thirties, neatly dressed, totally nonthreatening posture. Hands at his sides—no evidence of a weapon. "Yes?"

"I'll be your driver this evening, ma'am," he continued, taking a few steps toward a white limousine idling at the curb. "If you'll allow me." He reached to open the rear door.

"You've made a mistake," Rian informed him, shaking her head.

He smiled and handed her an envelope. "No, ma'am." He remained by the open door, patiently waiting.

Frowning, Rian opened the envelope, pulled out a cream-colored card, and read the familiar bold script.

Remember the time at your mother's with your sister in the next room? You cried when you came. You were so beautiful. Come to me tonight.

Rian colored involuntarily at the recollection of trying desperately to be quiet, a pillow clenched firmly in her teeth, as Bren stroked her gently but relentlessly to a climax. The note could only be from her. Rian looked at the man beside the vehicle, searching for any hint of danger, anything that didn't feel right. He smiled benignly; she laughed quietly and slid into the luxurious interior. Sometimes a rose *is* just a rose.

The dark leather smell surrounded her, and on the seat she found a real rose with a small white card pinned to its stem.

Have I told you today how much I love you?
Let me tell you now...
More, my darling, than I can ever say.

Rian read the words again, at once warmed and mystified, still unable to believe the changes in her life since Bren. She had never expected this love—never sought it, nor dreamed it, nor longed for it. And now she could not imagine living without it. *Without Bren.* The mere thought was physically painful. She held the card tightly, trying to see the street signs through the tinted windows in hopes of gleaning their destination. Logan Square—God, she hoped Bren hadn't planned anything too classy. She wasn't dressed for it, and she was bone tired. She had been working nonstop on one breaking story after another for weeks, and she was running on empty. Still, the thrill of anticipation had her rapidly forgetting her fatigue.

A few moments later, the limo slowed, and her heart plummeted.

Oh, God—not the Four Seasons! I am absolutely not prepared for dinner there!

Her driver pulled around the curving drive to the entrance and hurried to open her door. To her surprise, he accompanied her into the spacious foyer with its high ceiling, vast marble floor, and Federal-era furnishings. To her relief, he steered her away from the Fountain dining room toward a private elevator tucked away in a corner. A dignified man in an elaborate, brocade-laden uniform stood by the open door.

"To the Presidential Suite, Henry," the driver said, then quietly slipped away.

"Madam," Henry said in a deep formal tone, gesturing for Rian to precede him into a beautiful elevator car adorned with plush wall coverings and dark walnut wainscoting.

Rian smiled at the appellation as she entered. The car rose with the barest whisper of motion and glided soundlessly to a stop. She stepped out into a private foyer carpeted in thick broadloom with Wedgwood-blue wallpaper in a pattern of fine stripes and a Sheraton table against one wall holding a vase of long-stem white roses. The elevator door swished closed just as the single door opposite opened.

Bren, obviously freshly showered and wearing a royal blue silk dressing gown that Rian had given her for Christmas, stood framed in the soft yellow glow cast by the shaded lamps in the room beyond. Her legs were bare below midthigh, where the robe ended, and Rian was quite certain that there was nothing but the sash and smooth cool silk over satin skin above that point.

"I see you got my message." Bren's voice was deep and sensuous, her smile slow and dangerous. Her dark hair was combed straight back from a face that made angels weep. Strong jaw, deep-set dark eyes, and a mouth made for pleasure.

"I don't know what to say," Rian admitted, walking forward to the threshold of an enormous suite of rooms. She felt shy for no reason that she could imagine. This was the woman who had held her countless nights and touched not just her body, but her life, more intimately than any other person ever had. Yet seeing her now, so absolutely stunning, Rian had a moment's insecurity. They had made love dozens of times, but she had never before been quite so aware of Bren's sexual magnetism.

Why me? Why do you want me?

"You don't have to say anything," Bren said quietly, extending her hand and drawing Rian into the suite. Standing behind Rian, she took her briefcase and set it down, lifted off her overcoat and laid it on a nearby sofa, and nuzzled her face in the crook of Rian's neck. Inhaling deeply, her hands just skimming Rian's arms, she murmured, "Mmm. You smell so good."

The warm breath caressed her ear, and Rian shivered.

"Cold?"

A soft mouth traveled down the column of her neck and back up again, lingering to gently suck her earlobe between hot, clever lips.

"No," Rian sighed. "Melting."

Bren chuckled and slid an arm around Rian's waist. "Come with me."

Bren led her to the bedroom where a king-sized bed, its ivory coverlet thrown back to reveal pale blue satin sheets and a mountain of pillows, dominated the room. A silver ice bucket stood nearby with a chilled bottle of Dom Perignon. The surroundings were opulent, the atmosphere hopelessly sensual, but it was the woman—the woman whose touch ignited her every sense—that held Rian enthralled. Every time with Bren was like the first time—aching anticipation combined with dizzying desire. She turned and threaded her arms around Bren's neck.

"I should've known you wouldn't forget."

"You're all I thought about all day." Bren dipped her head and pressed her lips to the hollow at the base of Rian's throat. She touched the rippling pulse point with the tip of her tongue, then sucked the tender skin until Rian whimpered. "You're all I think about *every* day."

"I've missed you." Rian arched into Bren as her muscles and nerves tightened, her skin burning with the relentless rise of arousal. With the fingers of one hand tangled in the damp, thick hair at the nape of Bren's neck, she slid her other hand between them and pulled on the sash at Bren's waist. Bren quickly caught her hand and prevented her from opening the robe.

"What—?" Rian protested.

"Wait. There's more."

More. There's always more with you. More tenderness, more patience, more understanding...so much more than I ever imagined.

"Oh," Rian moaned as Bren very slowly and very gently removed each article of her clothing. As each button was loosed, each barrier shed, Bren stroked the newly exposed skin with her fingers and her mouth. Neither of them spoke, but by the time Rian stood nude before her lover, they were both flushed and Rian was trembling. Bren wrapped her in a white chenille robe, held her close with an encircling arm, and poured two glasses of champagne with her free hand. She handed one flute to Rian and lifted the other in a small salute.

"I plan on spoiling you tonight," Bren said, her voice husky with promise. She opened the door to the bathroom and drew Rian inside. A huge sunken tub was filled to the top with steaming water. Rose petals floated on the surface amidst the delicate suds from a scented bath gel. The air was heavy with their mingled perfume, suffusing Rian with a languid sense of ripe sensuality.

"I just filled the tub, so the water is still hot." Bren eased the robe from Rian's shoulders and guided her to the single stair and down into the bath.

Rian slid into the silky, soothing water, groaning as the knots of tension in her muscles relaxed. She leaned her head back against the contoured edge of the tub and surveyed Bren through half-closed eyelids. "I'm appropriately spoiled."

"Not just yet you're not." Bren settled a hip on the broad rim of the tub and lifted the crystal champagne flute to her lips while casting an admiring glance over the creamy expanse of shoulders and curve of breasts exposed above the light layer of suds. A faint sheen of perspiration misted Rian's lips, and she leaned forward to brush the tiny droplets away with a kiss. When she spoke against Rian's mouth, her voice was tight. "You're so beautiful. I want to touch you everywhere." She put her champagne aside. "Let me bathe you."

Rian smiled slowly and held out her hand. "Join me."

"Mmm, soon," Bren replied, slipping out of her robe before reaching for a large, soft sponge. She scooped up the fragrant suds and began to lightly massage Rian's arms and shoulders.

Rian groaned again, arching her body upward, her breasts emerging from the water pink from the warmth, nipples puckering in the cooler air. She looked at Bren's handsome face bending near and felt the dark intensity of her lover's eyes on her skin. She recognized the desire swirling there. And she asked a question she had never asked before, not even sure why she needed to know. "Why do you love me?"

Bren's eyes grew pensive as she traced one finger down the outer edge of Rian's breast. She brushed her palms over Rian's breasts, lingering a mere instant on her nipples, teasing out a soft moan.

"The first time I saw you, I knew I had never seen anyone like you before." She returned to Rian's breasts, lifting them softly in her hands, thumb and forefinger squeezing the tense nipples. Rian bit her bottom lip and pushed into Bren's hands. Bren continued, her voice dreamy. "Your eyes are so fierce, and so tender. Your face is so strong, and terribly gentle. Your beauty makes my heart ache."

"Bren," Rian murmured helplessly.

"The first time I touched you, I knew I had never touched anyone as desirable as you." Bren glided her hands under the surface of the water and beneath Rian's legs. She began to slowly knead the calves, working her fingers deeply into the taut muscles. She reached Rian's feet, her deft surgeon's hands massaging the fine bones and tendons rhythmically.

Rian groaned, sinking deeper into the warmth, seduced by the intoxicating pleasure of Bren's ministrations.

"You excite me as no one ever has," Bren whispered. She stroked the length of each toe, rubbing the pads with her thumbs. "You make me weak with wanting you."

Rian slowly opened her eyes only to find her vision blurred by desire. Her body was humming, her blood racing with need. She brushed one hand unconsciously over her breasts. They throbbed to be touched, and she flicked her nipple with one finger. Her stomach clenched as the electricity streaked down into her thighs. "I want you next to me."

"Soon." Bren edged her legs into the tub and smoothed the fingers of both hands up the inside of Rian's legs. She made teasing circles over the sleek inner thighs, gliding on the soap-softened skin, reaching higher with each pass. Her fingers glanced over soft curls, and Rian cried out. "You are every dream I have ever dared dream."

Words spoken so softly they were like another caress.

"Now, please." Rian lifted her hips, sending small ripples across the surface of the water. "I need you to touch me. I need you so much."

Silently, Bren slipped into the water and moved behind Rian to cradle her in her arms. She nestled her cheek to Rian's, pressed her breasts against Rian's back, and cupped her palms beneath Rian's breasts. "I'm here. I'll always be here."

"Promise."

"Swear."

"Good." Rian leaned her head back against Bren's chest, curled her fingers around the strong arms that encircled her, and guided the broad hands down over her belly. She led Bren's fingers between her thighs, her breath catching as she felt the first exquisite touch. "Oh. There. That's so nice," she breathed. "I never would have believed anyone could do this to me. You own my soul."

"You," Bren whispered, her lips against Rian's neck, "are my heart's desire." She closed her eyes as she slipped her fingers slowly into Rian's warm depths, groaning quietly as she was immediately enclosed in the velvet grip. With her other hand, she caressed the firm clitoris.

Rian's legs tightened and her hips rocked, creating currents in the water that ebbed and flowed around them, keeping time with Bren's long, smooth strokes. Her breath grew ragged and short as her senses spiraled down to center in the nerve endings sparking deep within her. Blood pounded and pulsed through her belly, her muscles quivered, and her heart thudded erratically. She was so very close, and so very ready.

"I'm going to come for you," Rian gasped. She closed her fingers hard around Bren's wrist, pressing the hand inside her deeper still, riding the tantalizing length of those fingers as Bren's palm massaged her stiff clitoris. She teased her own nipples, igniting the first wisps of orgasm. "Oh, yes. I am. I am."

"I can feel you coming," Bren murmured in wonder. "Oh, God, I can feel you, baby."

Rian crooned her delight, small sighs and murmurs that blended and grew louder as she neared the point where consciousness shatters and sensation rules. With one deep tremor she succumbed, shuddering repeatedly within the safe circle of Bren's embrace. Tears mixed with the warm mist on her cheeks.

They clung to each other, lost for words to express the wonder they had found together.

Until, "I love you so much."

Two voices, one eternal passion.

STAGESTRUCK

There's nothing quite so lonely as a Saturday night in a strange town on the far side of midnight. In the last twenty-four hours, I'd crossed more than just time zones and thousands of miles—I'd shed one reality for another, let my ordinary life slip away like an unneeded cloak until I arrived halfway around the world a different person. No one knew me other than as the persona I allowed them to see. No one met me at the airport, because I wasn't scheduled to appear until the next morning. Until then, I was only a name on a program and a face on a flyer.

Too tired to sleep and too restless to read, I decided to go for a walk, ignoring the concerned expression on the night clerk's face as I crossed the lobby and stepped out into the dark. As was true in so many cities in the middle of the night, traffic was sparse and pedestrians rare. Nevertheless, the sidewalks were well lit by a combination of streetlamps, neon reflections from store signs, and a surprisingly bright gibbous moon.

I walked in the direction that the cars were headed, the steady thud of my booted feet on the empty pavement a welcome accompaniment, like the beating of another heart in a darkened room. As soon as I turned the corner, I saw the bold, black letters of the stark white marquee a block away. *Grand Hotel.* Why not? What better way to spend the last hours of anonymity than with the woman who was famous for her secretiveness and seclusion. As I approached the theater, I caught movement out of the corner of my eye and turned to see a woman crossing the street at an angle, her path on an intercept with mine. With the lights behind her and her body shrouded in a long military-style coat that came to just below her knees, I could see little of her face and nothing of her body. I knew without doubt, however, that it *was* a woman by the singularly fluid grace of her movements. She drew near with a purposeful stride as if she were late to meet me and eager to catch up. I slowed to wait, as if our rendezvous were prearranged.

"Are you going to the theater?"

Her voice was husky, with a lilting accent that tinged her English with a hint of Scandinavia. Closer now, I could see that she was indeed blond, her eyes blue or green, too muted in the half-light for me to be certain. Her coat billowed with each step, exposing long legs in pale denim and a shirt unbuttoned far enough to reveal that she wore nothing under it.

"Yes. Do you think it's too late?"

"No," she replied, extending her hand. "I think we're just in time."

I took her hand as if I had a hundred times before.

Her fingers were long, slender, and cool. Her palm was soft, but with a faint ridge at the base of each finger suggesting that she worked with her hands. I stole another glance at her face, thinking that with her arched cheekbones and full jaw she might have been a model. But there was nothing studied or posed about her. She was at ease in her body in a way that those who made their living with theirs were not.

"Have you seen it before?" I asked.

Her full mouth curved into a secret smile. "Many times."

She moved even closer as we walked until her shoulder and thigh touched mine, the way a lover's would, with familiarity and possession. I struggled not to close my fingers tightly around hers as a surge of desire caught me unawares and made me stumble.

"Are you all right?" she asked.

"Perfect," I replied, only then realizing that it was true. At the first touch of her hand, I'd forgotten the disquieting sensation of being halfway around the world and a stranger to everyone, even myself. The parts of myself I'd left behind slowly reappeared, sliding into the empty places effortlessly until I remembered who I was and why I had come.

"Two, please," she announced as she passed several oddly colored notes through the semicircular hole in the Plexiglas to the bored-looking young man in the booth.

"Oh no," I protested, belatedly realizing that we had reached the theater while I had been lost somewhere between yesterday and tomorrow. "You must let me pay."

She laughed softly. "It is, as you would say, my treat."

I blushed furiously, not at all certain that she meant it the way I took it, but her words brought another flood of arousal from my depths. She cocked an eyebrow at me, then swept her fingers lightly over my cheek and down my neck until her hand cupped my throat. She leaned close, there in the bright lights of the ticket booth, and skimmed her mouth over mine. "We should go in."

"Yes," I breathed, wanting nothing more than more of her mouth.

The lights went down just as we stepped into the theater, and she guided me through the blackness into the back row, to the far corner seats. There was no one in front of us or to the side. In fact, the other figures in the room were merely faint reminders that we were not alone. Distant images of Garbo and Barrymore flickered on the screen, their words a faint hum beneath the roaring in my ears.

Her coat fanned out behind her as she shrugged it from her shoulders, and when she extended her arm along the seat behind my back, the tips of her fingers grazed my shoulder. Each fleshy circle was a burning coal that penetrated the cotton to my skin. I leaned against her, and when my breast pressed to her side, my nipple tightened into a pebble of tingling nerves. She curled her arm and drew me closer, shifting to put her mouth against my ear.

"No one can see."

It wasn't true, but the illusion of invisibility beneath the otherworldly light in the cavernous space was enough. I tugged the shirt from her jeans and rested my hand on her belly. Her stomach tensed as I slowly rubbed my palm over the soft skin, pressing harder as the moments passed, my eyes on the screen but every sense tuned to her. The muscles beneath my fingers quivered and grew rigid, and with a faint moan, she shifted in her seat and spread her legs wide, her knee brushing mine. I knew she would be naked under the denim. The fingers that curved around my upper arm trembled. I could stop, but what would be the point? From the instant she'd taken my hand and I'd let her, our destination had been clear.

It was my turn to skim my lips over her ear, my breath a teasing kiss. "Are you hard already? Can you feel the seam brush against your clit, just like my lips caressing the tip?"

"Yes." Urgent and low.

My hand moved up, pushing fabric aside to cup her breast, grasping a nipple—already standing up, hard and sensitive, waiting. I squeezed gently. Once more. And again, harder, twisting a little until her body stiffened and another soft gasp escaped her. Her hips lifted, her heart skittering beneath my palm. I lowered my mouth to the other breast, biting through the soft cotton to tug on tender flesh. The gasp became a moan - hers or mine, I wasn't certain. My clit jerked insistently, keeping time with her racing pulse, and I finally dropped my free hand to my crotch and rubbed the stiff prominence through my pants.

"Open your jeans," I murmured against her neck as I drew my tongue along the curve of that beautiful jaw. Her breath, shallow and fast, drowned out the sound of Crawford's haughty inflections. I glanced down, saw her rip at the button and zipper, and squeezed the fabric between my thighs hard around my own aching need. My clit twitched, my vision blurred, and I had to ease off or come. I tortured her nipple a little more with my teeth to take my mind off the pressure in my clit.

Her eyes, suddenly bright and clear in the murky light, held mine.

"Please."

I stopped touching myself and pushed my fingers down the front of her pants as she rocked her hips, urging my fingers to find her. God, I wanted to take her fast—to make her come on my fingers, in my hand. I rested my fingertips just above the base of her clitoris, pressing down ever more firmly while circling up and down the stiff length, making it throb as the blood built inside. I knew how it felt, how it hurt in a way that could only be pleasure. Then, one hand stroking through that liquid heat below, I grasped her neck with my free hand and turned her face to mine. I worked my tongue into her mouth, the way I wanted to be working inside her. Turning in the seat, I threw one leg over hers. Clit pounding as I rode her leg, I sucked on her tongue the way I wanted her sucking on me. She bucked on my hand and moaned into my mouth and I forgot why I was waiting. Her need and mine conspired to undo me, and I surrendered willingly.

I pushed my hand deeper into her pants, my wrist tenting the denim until the zipper bit into my skin. Unmindful of the pain, I slid my fingers into her and angled my arm to get higher, crushing her clit, wet and hard, into my palm. Half lying on her now, my tongue in her mouth, my fingers buried inside, I took her hard and fast, beating her clit with the heel of my hand on each thrust. She pulled away from the kiss and closed her teeth on my neck when she started to come, muffling her cries with my flesh. She clamped down around my fingers as her hips jerked up, her rigid body barely touching the seat, and I felt a breathless, heart-stopping wonder as she came. I was ready to come, needed desperately to come, but in that moment, the only thing that I knew was her pleasure. Only when she slumped back into the seat with a last, long moan did the fury of my desire overtake me. I closed my hand around her still-pulsing sex and lowered my forehead to her chest. Dimly I was aware of her holding me as I shuddered and thrust against her tensed thigh. I choked on my own sobs of pleasure as a dam burst inside me and every barrier dissolved. I came in the arms of a stranger who knew me more intimately in that moment than anyone else in my life.

We dozed through the rest of the movie. I blamed my torpor on jet lag, but the truth was that I liked the way she held me. When the credits rolled, we straightened our clothing and left before the others. The streets were completely empty, and we walked in silence the few short blocks to my hotel. In the darkness beneath the awning, she leaned down and kissed me, the same knowing brush of lips with which she had first greeted me.

"Good night," she said softly.

I watched her walk away until the billowing edges of her coat became only the shifting shadows of the night. Then I turned and walked inside. It was not the Grand Hotel, and no grand passion awaited me here. But when I finally lay my head upon the crisp, white pillowcase, I felt her body next to mine and her breath against my cheek. I closed my eyes, knowing I would not sleep alone.

FOUR-STAR ACCOMMODATIONS

W hen you pay $300 a night for a room, you expect a little something in the way of special service. This place provided it, in spades. The historic inn had been carefully renovated and every amenity tended to. I knew, because I'd stayed there before, and I appreciated the bed turn-down each night, the small silver-foil-wrapped chocolates on my pillow, the complimentary full breakfast with endless coffee, and the pleasant wait staff.

Unfortunately, I arrived in less than good humor after having been rerouted on my flight not once but twice, because of mechanical problems with the aircraft. It was nearly 10:00 p.m., I'd been dragging heavy luggage around for hours, and I was, to put it mildly, cranky. When the cab let me off in the gravel drive, I hoisted my suitcases up the four wooden stairs to the office and unceremoniously dumped them in the foyer. The reception desk was tucked into a nook on one side of the anteroom, and beyond it, I could see the sitting area with its thick carpets, lace curtains, and antique sofas and chairs. It was tastefully elegant and undeniably beautiful.

The real eye-catcher, though, stood behind the counter. Five feet ten or so of blond-haired, blue-eyed, all-American Dyke. Those sparkling indigo eyes were set off perfectly by the tight navy blue T-shirt that stretched across small breasts and nicely muscled shoulders. She leaned on the counter, her bare forearms tanned and solid. She had big hands, strong hands, with long fingers that looked capable of almost anything. Her smile was slow and easy, and I felt my mood shift from aggravated to intrigued.

"Hi," I said, sliding my wallet from my back pocket.

"You must be Parker," she said without benefit of checking the guest list.

Impressed, I nodded and handed her my credit card. "That would be me."

"Long flight?"

I grimaced. "Long, hot, and crowded."

As we spoke, she efficiently ran my card, printed out my reservation, and passed the paper to me across the countertop. "Sign here."

As I did, she handed me a cream-colored brochure announcing the inn's newest offering—a full-service spa providing facials, Swedish massage, deep muscle therapy, and any number of other body-pampering treatments. I skimmed it quickly and groaned with sudden desire. "I don't suppose there's anyone available now, is there? After the day I've had, a massage sounds perfect."

After the briefest hesitation, she shook her head. "Sorry. I can make you a reservation for the morning, if that will help."

I shrugged. "That's okay. Maybe a shower and a decent night's sleep will take care of it."

"Well, if you change your mind," she said, stepping around the counter to join me, "be sure to ask for Wes."

"Is he good?"

She reached for my larger bag, hefted it easily, and grinned. "*She* would be me, and yes, I am."

"I take it that massage therapy is your day job?" I grinned back as I gathered the rest of my luggage.

"Afternoon and evening job."

Wes led the way through a carefully landscaped rear garden to one of the smaller guest cottages. My room had a small private porch, complete with a circular wrought-iron table and matching chairs. I opened the door to a lushly appointed guest room with a king-sized bed, carved wooden headboard, matching side tables, and spindle-legged desk against one wall.

"God, I love this place," I murmured.

"Glad to hear it."

I turned, my knees almost touching the foot of the large bed, and studied her as she stood just inside the doorway, my luggage at her feet. She was easy to look at, and I had a sudden image of lying facedown on the massage table, a thin strip of sheet covering my butt and the rest of my body bare. It wasn't hard to imagine those capable-looking hands on my skin, kneading muscles and manipulating tendons. I loved to be massaged, loved the attention. I always found it a little bit arousing, but I'd never found myself in one of those situations that are so easy to fantasize about. A massage had always been just a massage. Still, the look of her did set my mind to wandering down steamy paths. It wasn't altogether surprising to find her studying me. We were, after all, both lesbians.

"So, Wes," I said softly. "Will you be available tomorrow for a session?"

She nodded, her eyes flickering down my body. "Uh-huh. Three to eight."

"I'll call in the morning—do you do ninety-minute sessions?"

Her eyes, dark as midnight now, returned to mine. "I'll do anything you want."

That produced an all-over clench—thighs, belly, groin. Suddenly, I wasn't tired any longer. She had sturdy legs agreeably displayed in her nearly threadbare khakis, and I had another flash of her straddling me as she worked the muscles along my spine. I imagined lifting my butt into her crotch ever so subtly, and the instant I visualized it, I was wet. I wanted to say, *You have no idea what I want*, but I wasn't entirely certain she meant it the way I had taken it. My hormones were in overdrive, but that didn't mean that hers were.

"I'll remember that," I replied, trying to sound nonchalant.

We stared at each other for another minute, and then she backed out the door, her eyes still on mine. "Well then. Good night."

"Good night."

I watched the door swing closed, heard the lock click, and imagined I felt the vibrations of her footsteps on the wooden deck as she disappeared. I slowly turned in a circle and surveyed the room. The prospect of unpacking held little appeal. I opened a suitcase, pulled out a long, nearly disintegrating cotton T-shirt I'd had since college and of which I was absurdly fond, and carried it into the bathroom. Within seconds, I was standing under a warm spray, soaping my body and fantasizing that my hands were hers.

I succeeded in washing away the stressful sweat of a long day and awakening my slumbering libido. By the time I had toweled dry and pulled on the T-shirt, I was thoroughly aroused and contemplating sliding beneath the sheets and masturbating. I'd be temporarily satisfied, I'd be relaxed, and I'd be able to sleep.

As I made my way toward the bed, I was startled by a soft knock at the door. The clock on the bedside table said 11:05 p.m. At the door, I fingered the blinds aside and peered out to see Wes standing on the deck, a tray in her hands and a slightly uncertain smile on her face. Immediately, I pulled open the door.

"Hey."

She lifted the tray in my direction, and I could see now that it held several towels and a bottle of what appeared to be massage oil.

"On the house."

My already tense clitoris gave a jump. I raised my eyes to hers and tilted my head consideringly. "What about the desk?"

"I'm off at 11:00."

I was about to get off myself. I had to force myself not to laugh at the timing, and held the door wide. "How can I possibly resist."

"I can't imagine," she said with considerably more confidence as she stepped inside.

"On the bed?" I questioned, glancing quickly about the room. There really wasn't any other choice unless I wanted to climb up on the narrow desk, which somehow I did not think was designed for massage.

"Yes."

Her tone was completely professional as she turned away to set the tray beside the bed and rearrange her implements. "It's best if you disrobe." Blindly, she held a towel in my direction. "Just put this across your middle, from your breasts to your thighs." There was a moment's hesitation during which she still did not look at me. "If you want."

"And if I don't?" I asked softly.

She turned then and met my eyes, hers steady and warm. "That would be fine too."

Slowly I reached down, grasped the hem of my T-shirt, and pulled it off over my head. Naked, I waited while she very slowly lowered her gaze, taking her time as she surveyed me. I felt a flush that might have been arousal or self-consciousness warm my skin, but the expression of pleasure on her face quickly banished any uncertainty. "Stomach or back?"

Her voice sounded scratchy and thick as she murmured, "I'd like it if you'd face me."

"Then I will." I settled on my back on the bed, my head on the pillow, my hands by my sides, and my legs slightly parted. "You're going to have to get up here with me to do this."

"I know."

She stood at the foot of the bed, waiting. Then I realized why.

"You'll be more comfortable if you take your clothes off too."

Her breath caught audibly, but she immediately unbuttoned her khakis, pulled her shirt from beneath the waistband and over her head, and dropped it behind her. She wore no bra, and her breasts, as I expected, were small and firm and high. Beautifully curved against the flat planes of her chest and belly. Then her strong hands were pushing down her pants and underwear, exposing the soft blond triangle at the apex of her sturdy thighs. I ached to look at her.

A second later, she had grasped the bottle of massage oil, climbed onto the bed, and knelt astride me. The insides of her thighs just brushed the outside of my hips, and her center hovered a breath above mine. I was wet and enormously aroused, and I knew my erect clitoris would be clearly visible if she looked down. If she lowered herself only a fraction, I would be enclosed within her sex. I was in danger of coming just from the thought.

"The oil's warm," she murmured as she squeezed the golden liquid into her palm. She set the bottle aside, rubbed her hands together until they glistened in the lamplight, then leaned down and pressed her palms into the center of my chest.

My nipples were instantly hard and impossible to hide. I held myself as still as I could, but I felt every one of my muscles contract at once. Her touch was firm and sure as she stroked her fingertips the length of my collarbone, then circled over my pectoral muscles and down the center of my sternum to my belly. As she worked, repeating the cycle, pressing and probing and smoothing my flesh, she rocked back and forth in a slow arc above me. Through eyes glazed with pleasure, I watched the muscles in her arms ripple and her small breasts sway. I felt a trickle of moisture on my leg and realized it was her sweat dripping from her thigh to mine. I caught my lip to stifle a moan.

"Feel good?"

Her voice was husky, low, with the barest hint of a tremor. I looked down her body and saw her abdomen tense just as she brushed her moist center ever so lightly against my stomach. She was hot and wet and I felt her thighs tremble. My breath caught. So did hers.

"Wonderful." I moved my hands to her legs, resting my thumbs in the cleft between her abdomen and thighs, my fingers splayed on the taut muscles. "You're a little tight yourself."

"Long day." She smiled crookedly and fanned her fingers lightly over my nipples.

The shock of pleasure was so acute I gasped aloud and dug my fingers into her thighs. Her body jerked beneath my hands, and she closed her eyes with a grimace.

"Hurt?" I murmured.

Shaking her head, she opened her eyes, her breath shallow and fast. "No. Good."

I realized then what my own pleasure at her touch had blinded me to before. She was trembling, her skin was hot beneath my hands, and rivulets of perspiration streaked her chest and abdomen. She was on fire, and suddenly, so was I. Without another thought, I put both hands on her waist, thrust my hips, and turned her over. She didn't protest. Then my mouth was on hers, she was pulling my tongue inside, and her legs were wrapping around my hips.

My skin was slick with oil, hers with sweat. We were both wet with excitement, and we slid against each other, grasping and groaning and hungry. Small, choked sounds of desperate pleasure escaped her throat, and I was forced to put my teeth against her skin to taste her desire. She arched her neck, allowing me to feast. I bit her lightly; her nails pressed crescents of passion into my back. Then her strong, capable hands closed around my shoulders and her long, tight abdomen contracted as she half sat up and pushed me down. She braced herself on both arms and looked down as my face came to rest between her thighs.

"I want to watch you make me come," she whispered.

Desire twisting through me, I took her with my mouth, not gently, knowing instinctively how she wanted it. Murmuring, "Oh yes, suck me, suck me," she pushed into me, forcing her clitoris to slide in and out between my lips, relentless and demanding. Somehow, she held herself upright even as I felt her orgasm gathering. Her thighs shook as they enclosed my body, and a thin, keening cry escaped her. She was close, on the verge, and I could wait no longer. I caressed my fingers up the inside of her thigh and into her, never interrupting the motion of my tongue against her clitoris. She came instantly into my hand, her body wracked with spasms. Finally, her strength gave out and she collapsed backward, still quivering in my mouth.

Despite my own painful arousal, I could not let her go. Licking her softly, I closed my fingers around my clitoris, needing only a few well-placed strokes to bring myself to orgasm. I sighed and moaned against her and felt her grow hard again between my lips. Still coming, I sucked her and heard her cry out. Then her hands were pushing me away.

"Can't. God. Enough." She laughed. "So good."

Laughing now too, I fell over onto my back, one arm curled over her thigh as I stared at the ceiling and fought for breath. The sound of her contented sighs lulled me to sleep, and I was not aware of her leaving.

I awoke naked, covered by the sheet, with that incredible looseness in body and mind that spoke of excellent loving. I turned my head, not surprised to see that the tray and towels and massage oil were gone. Sighing with more than a hint of disappointment, I contemplated rousing myself for the excellent breakfast that was probably now being served. Somehow, the prospect of dressing and walking seemed too much effort. I preferred to lie in bed, replay the pleasures of the evening, and perhaps recreate some of that excitement as I did so.

I had just smoothed my fingers down my abdomen when the knock sounded at the door. Frowning, I double-checked the clock. Eight thirty in the morning was far too early for housekeeping. I called out "Who is it?" with more than a little aggravation.

"Room service."

That was one amenity I hadn't been aware of, and I hastily pulled on a robe and made my way to the door. When I pulled it open, Wes stood there with a tray in her hands, a crooked grin on her face.

"And this would be what?" I asked. "Your morning job?"

"Seven to three." Her grin widened. "You ordered breakfast?"

I reached out, hooked my fingers over the waistband of her black jeans, and tugged her inside. Just before my mouth covered hers, I answered, "Yes. The house special."

SURPRISE PARTY

"Where are we going?"
"Be patient. It's a surprise."
"Oh, come on—tell me."

She gave me that winning grin, the one where just the corner of her mouth tilts up while her eyes dance on the cusp of mischief and longing. I could have fallen for that smile, those baby doe eyes, that fresh-faced innocent charm. I probably would have, if we hadn't been best buddies since we were ten years old. Growing up, we'd played softball together, discovered our mutual passion for girls together, and eventually experienced "the real deal" within weeks of each other. We'd been together in every way that mattered, except one. Since we both considered ourselves to be studs, well, it just wouldn't be right. So, as much as that curve of full lips and tiny dimple just off to the side got to me, I was determined to resist the allure. After all, making her wait was the whole point. "Uh-uh. No hints."

She bumped my shoulder, looked tough. "Tell me, or I won't tell *you* about the next time I get laid."

That threat didn't work. She oughtta know *I* knew she'd suffer just as much as me if she couldn't share her sexcapades. I think we *both* knew that there was more pleasure in watching the other get turned on by the blow-by-blow reruns than in doing it in the first place. Sometimes we did a little more than just talk about what went down with other women—sometimes we watched each other get off while we replayed it. I think we were both scared to think about what that meant, too, or why sometimes—just maybe—we thought about each other when we were doing strangers. I wasn't going *there,* for sure.

So I just shrugged and looked tough back. "Listen—you said I could have anything I wanted for my birthday, right?"

"Well, yeah."

"Okay—so this is it."

"*What* is *it?* Aren't I supposed to be giving *you* the present?"

"You will be." Something of my need must have shown in my face, because her grin vanished and her eyes grew soft, almost liquid. She lifted a hand, nearly touched my cheek before pulling her hand abruptly back and stuffing it into the pocket of her cracked and worn brown bomber jacket.

"Right." Her voice was husky, and she covered up that brief moment of vulnerability by pointing to my gym bag. "So what's in there?"

Now it was my turn to grin as I just shook my head and kept silent. When she swore, I laughed. Man, she was easy.

A moment later, we reached the place, a nondescript three-story wood house on a nondescript block in a totally forgettable part of the city. We climbed the stairs side by side, but before I rang the bell, I looked her in the eye. And this time, she knew I wasn't playing.

"You trust me, right?"

She held my gaze, her expression totally serious—a very rare thing for her. "With everything I am."

My heart tripped at the words, at the look of near devotion on her face, but I put those feelings away. We weren't ready to go there either, probably never would be. But there were other places we could go together. "Okay then. No matter what happens, no matter what anyone does, it's just us, okay?"

"Okay."

"*You* do what I say."

"Right."

"*Anything* I say."

She swallowed hard but nodded with absolute certainty. Absolute trust. "Yes."

Satisfied, my stomach jumping with nerves and excitement, I rang.

The lady of the house answered the door in a red, slinky robe-kinda thing that covered the essentials, but just barely. Nice essentials, too; firm full breasts—only a suggestive slice of pale flesh beneath smooth silk now—narrow waist, and strong hips you could hold on to when the ride got rough.

She smiled at me, a smile that said, "I know just what you want." And she did. I'd been there before, but my buddy didn't know that. As close as we were, there were still some secrets I hadn't shared. After tonight, there'd be one less.

"Right on time, just like always." The lady's voice was whiskey warm and never failed to give me a rush. Still standing in the doorway, one hip cocked, her full lips pursed, she gave my buddy a long, slow survey and made a little purring sound in the back of her throat. Like she was hungry and had just spied a feast. "Mmm. Nice."

My buddy blushed and damn near shuffled her feet. She's very fucking cute when she does that.

With another little hum of approval, our hostess turned and led the way into the mostly dark house. Silently, we followed her up two flights of stairs and down a narrow hallway into a room with a plush Oriental carpet, two wide leather armchairs set at angles to each other, and a smattering of other furniture against the walls. The lights, focused in a soft circle just around the chairs, were turned down low, but anyone sitting in one could clearly see the person in the other.

"Don't hurry," the lady said as she left us, pulling the door nearly but not quite closed.

"What—" my buddy began.

"Wait." My voice sounded husky to my own ears. Jesus, I was so turned on already I was almost sick with the craving in my belly.

I unbuttoned my shirt while she watched, curiosity and the beginnings of desire flaring in her eyes. I had nothing on beneath the shirt, and once bare, my nipples tightened instantly into small, hard knots. I kicked off my boots and socks, unbuttoned my jeans, and stripped them off. I hadn't worn anything under *them* either. Her hot gaze slid down my body and back up, ending on my face. The heat from her stare made me hard. It always did.

"Your turn," I said quietly.

She repeated my actions, all the while watching *me* watch *her*, until she stood naked and exposed in the soft, yellow light. Her small firm breasts rose and fell quickly with the rush of breath in and out of her lungs. She shivered, and it wasn't because she was cold. I felt the first trickle of wetness on my thigh. Before my legs shook too badly, I sat in one chair and gestured to the other. She sat.

With her attention riveted to me, I spread my legs and ran a hand down the center of my body, along the inside of one thigh, then the other. Then, taking my time, I drew one hand between my legs, used my fingers to open myself, and flicked a fingertip against the base of my clit. My stomach clutched just as her breath caught in her throat.

"Can you see it?" My voice was hoarse. Christ, I was so stiff already I was afraid I wouldn't last.

"Yeah. Oh, yeah."

My clit was screaming. I forced myself to pull my hand away. I could tell she wanted to finger herself but she wasn't sure if she was allowed. Her legs were already tight, the way they got when she was wicked hard and wanted to come. It was going to be a long, long night.

"Go ahead," I said softly. "Stroke it a little. But go easy. You can't come until I tell you you can."

Her fingers flew to her clit. The muscles in her tight belly jumped. Her eyes, still fixed between my legs, got a little unfocused as she pressed back and forth on the spot where her clit joined her body.

"Let me see what you got," I demanded, lightly rubbing the end of my own hard-on now. The little bit of pressure made me ache as I smoothed hot come up and down the shaft.

Carefully, she skimmed back the hood. I saw her thigh muscles twitch. She was already big—wet—the head pulsing rhythmically. Oh, yeah, she was ready.

"Now," I whispered as the door opened soundlessly, "you watch."

The lady in red glided quietly across the floor and knelt before my chair, angling her body so that my buddy's view was unobstructed. She rested her cheek against the inside of my left thigh. I slid a finger on either side of my clit and squeezed. The stab of pleasure was so sharp I gasped. I heard my buddy draw a quick breath, too, a sob almost, and out of the corner of my eye, I saw the hand between her legs circling faster. I looked back down at myself, at the woman's face cradled against my leg.

"Jesus, I'm so hard I'm gonna explode." Trying to keep a lid on, I squeezed again. When I pulled back swollen flesh, the head popped out, dark and red and so sensitive I moaned. I glanced at my buddy again—she was pinching the tip of her clit softly, her dazed eyes on my fingers as I struggled to hold back my orgasm. That just made my clit jerk and swell more. Staring at her, I spoke quietly to the lady in red.

"Lick it slow." Bracing myself, I kept a grip on the shaft with two fingers, exposing the head for her. I looked down as the warm wet tongue slipped up the underside of my clit. I almost came with the first stroke. My insides were in knots, my legs so tight I was cramping. Jesus, I wanted to come so bad.

I realized my friend was pumping into her palm and breathing hard. "Feel good?" It was hard for me to talk because the lady was switching between tonguing the sides of my clit and sucking lightly on the head.

"Oh, fuck yeah. I'm gonna come all over my hand," she groaned, hips twisting, her stomach board tight.

"Uh-uh. No." I risked fucking my clit between those soft lips, but when I slid the length in and out, the top of my head almost came off. As much to myself as to her, I grunted, "Not yet."

"Can't hold it." She was gasping, her eyes glued to my clit, her fingers steadily tugging at herself. I saw her working her clit the way that amazing mouth worked mine.

"Sure...you can." I suddenly got very hard and knew I was about to blow off into that warm, wet mouth. I eased my fingers into the lady's hair and pushed her gently off me. "Sorry...uh...not just yet."

I could hardly see, but I knew she was smiling. Oh, yeah, she knew how to work me.

I slumped in the chair, twitching all over, and looked at my buddy. Her eyes were glazed, her clit standing up like a mountain between her trembling fingers.

"Get the cocks out of the bag," I said.

She almost couldn't stop jerking her clit, she was so close to letting loose, but she finally did as I ordered.

"Give me one." I held out my hand. "Put one in."

"It'll make me come," she groaned, her thumb pressed hard against the base of her clit, trying to hold back her orgasm.

"Do it slow, with me." I pushed the head in and watched her watch me do it. I lifted my hips and let it fill me. The cock shaft dragged over my clit, and I groaned. The pressure on my clit from inside doubled, then tripled, and I needed to get off so desperately I cried out. Biting my lip, I looked over and saw the cock buried deep inside her, saw the look of pleasure-pain on her face, saw how much she needed to come. I grinned.

"Jesus Christ," she gasped. "I have to come so bad...gonna come on this cock." She was pumping on it nice and slow, nice and deep.

"Me...too." I glanced down. My clit stood up, stone hard and jerking all on its own. The woman who knelt between my legs waited, still softly smiling. Barely able to speak, I whispered, "Suck me until I come."

When her mouth closed over me and she started sliding my clit in and out between her lips, licking the head in steady circles, I leaned back, turned my head, and watched my buddy jerk herself off. Her eyes were still on me, her fingers on her clit, the other hand fucking the cock in and out.

I watched her watch me get sucked off, watched her get ready to come, all the while my clit getting harder, the cock heavy inside me. I couldn't take it.

"Oh...oh, I'm gonna come in her mouth," I whimpered. My friend's hips jerked and she moaned, eyes moving between my face and the woman sucking me. The orgasm exploded under the tongue working my clit, crashed into my guts, slammed down my legs. I spasmed and twitched. "Oh...fuck. I'm coming." I looked into those eyes I'd loved my whole life. "Baby, I'm coming."

Seeing me come always makes her come. With a shout, she doubled forward, pumping hard on the cock, jerking hard on her clit.

"Oh yeah oh yeah oh yeah," we cried together.

Together.

FIRST DRAFT

Gayle let herself into the apartment, her early morning foray for breakfast completed, and saw her brand-new lover still at the computer where she'd been an hour before. Quietly, so as not to interrupt her concentration, Gayle headed for the kitchen and another cup of coffee. She stopped at the sound of the voice behind her.

"Hey, babe. I missed you."

Gayle raised an eyebrow, the bag of bagels in her hand forgotten as the low, seductive timbre of Thane's voice hit home. Hit hard and sweet and hot. "Oh yeah? I thought you were working."

"I was. But I was *thinking* about you."

"Oh." For a moment, Gayle wasn't certain what else to say. She wasn't exactly sure what the ground rules were or where the boundaries lay. She adored her new lover's fiction—she still couldn't believe she was sleeping with one of the hottest erotica writers around. But she wasn't entirely certain that access to Thane's writing was part of their new relationship.

"What?" Thane eyed the small line that creased the smooth skin between Gayle's brows. "You bothered that I got out of bed to write? Believe me, it wasn't because of the company. Last night was...outstanding."

Thane's grin fanned the flames that smoldered between Gayle's thighs. *That mouth is so talented, those lips so—* She could still feel the velvet pressure as Thane sucked the orgasm from her. Her clit twitched. She struggled for words, her belly twisting with urgency.

"No, of course I'm not bothered. I...I love your stuff. It's cool, really—that you were working on it here." She shrugged, her throat dry, her stomach tight. "It's just..."

"What then?" Thane rose and crossed the room. Leaning close, she rested her hands on Gayle's hips.

Gayle sighed shyly. "I'm curious."

"Ah." Thane kissed her. "Wanna read it?"

"Oh, yeah. Big time." She hesitated when she realized what Thane was offering. "Really? You sure you don't mind?"

"Gayle, babe, I'm a writer. I want *everyone* to read what I write." Laughing, Thane took Gayle's hand and led the way to the computer. Then she sat and patted her lap. "Sit here and have a look."

Private Pleasures - Innocence Abounds

It's not what you think. I'm innocent. I swear. At least, until a minute ago, I was innocent.

A minute ago we were naked together, turning each other in the warm spray—playfully fighting over who would get the shampoo first. I hadn't intended anything—really—I just wanted to run my soapy hands over your body, to wash your back. Ten *seconds* ago, even, I was innocent. Then...when I reached around you just now for the bath gel and our bodies collided...

Now, maybe I'm not so innocent.

Thane held very still, her cheek pressed against Gayle's breast, her eyes closed. She could hear Gayle's heart beating. In her mind, she saw the words she had written and, barely breathing, waited for judgment.

Absently, Gayle settled her hips more comfortably between Thane's spread legs, one arm around her lover's shoulders, toying with her hair. With the other hand, she scrolled.

Now our bodies brush lightly—skin against skin, belly to belly, thigh to thigh—the silken hair between our legs blending gently in the warm streams of water coursing over us. When I slip my arms around you to reach your back, our breasts meet. My nipples, instantly erect, slide over yours, sending pulsating shocks of pleasure straight down my spine. The flickering contact teases me, starts a tingling between my legs, but the fleeting pressure on the aching tips of my breasts is not hard enough, not long enough, for what I need.

Gayle's nipples tightened and her thigh muscles clenched. Instantly wet, she was agonizingly aware of Thane's mouth a breath away from her skin. She threaded her fingers more tightly into Thane's hair and unconsciously pressed her breast against her lover's face.

I secret a hand between us, find your nipple and squeeze—once, twice— before circling your breasts with my soapy fingers. The soft weight of you in my palm is an invitation to feast. My mouth is watering. Lifting both breasts so the soothing cascade rinses the soap away, I bend my head, lick the clear drops from the tight, hard tips, and drink your passion. You close your eyes and grasp my hips, pulling me tighter. Moaning, you push a muscled thigh between mine, arching your back as my teeth claim flesh. We reach for one another at the same time; I find your clitoris just as you touch mine. You stroke the length...

"I don't think I can read this with you so close to me," Gayle said, her voice husky and low. "It's wonderful, but all I can feel is you."

Eyes still closed, Thane nuzzled a nipple, found it hard and tight, and sucked on it through the soft, worn flannel. "Too late," she mumbled. "Keep going."

The teeth on Gayle's nipple sent blood roaring into her clitoris. Struggling to focus, she tried to follow the words.

```
    ...stroke the length of my clit,
working me steadily, tugging the
stiff core as I roll the length of you
lightly between my thumb and finger.
Legs spread, hips pumping slowly,
our soft sighs mingle. We mirror one
another's movements, speeding up,
pressing harder—each bringing the other
closer with every stroke, moaning now
on trembling legs. I search for your
lips, clinging to you, and our mouths
meet, tongues joining, sucking hard
on swollen lips. I'm so hard now, so
ready to shoot my...
```

"Oh yeah," Gayle moaned, hips lifting as her clitoris throbbed. She fumbled for Thane's hand, drawing it beneath the waistband of her sweatpants, pushing it between her thighs. "Feel what you've done to me."

Very lightly, Thane ran a single finger over Gayle's clitoris. "Mmm, so hard, aren't you, babe."

When the teasing caress disappeared, Gayle gave a strangled cry and pressed her hand over Thane's, forcing Thane's fingers hard onto her clit. "Oh, don't stop."

With her free hand, Thane opened a button on the flannel shirt, then two, then drew a taut nipple between her lips. Her mouth to Gayle's breast, Thane whispered, "Don't come until the end."

```
    I'm circling my hips on your hand—
it feels...
```

"So good."

...I can't bear it. *Please, oh please make me come.* You turn me away from the stream of water, kneeling quickly, both hands between my legs, opening me for your lips. I'm so full, so hard, so close to exploding—so ready to come. Your tongue presses into me, warm and sweet...

"Oh, yes, yes...right there. Yes. Oh, baby, yes. That's so good."

...pulling the pleasure from me on a flood of arousal. My back is against the shower wall as you lean into me, sweeping your tongue up the length of my clitoris...

"I'll come if you keep touching me there."

...making my head light and my stomach twist. I can feel you moving against my leg, wet and hard. You're moaning, swollen against my skin, and you make me want...

"Oh, baby, I want..."

...to come. You are rocking against me as you suck me now, both of us shuddering, straining...

"I'm so close, so close now."

Your fingers are inside me, your lips tugging at my clitoris...

"I need to come. I need..."

```
...your tongue working me back and
forth. I'm going to come soon. I won't
come until you say—but oh, God—I need
to. Tell me when I can come, tell me
when...
```

"I'm coming...coming..."

```
...soon, soon, please tell me, tell
me, tell me...
```

"Oh, God, baby...please, hold me."

"I'm right here. I won't let go."

"Oh, Jesus." Gayle clung to Thane, pressed her face to Thane's neck, trembling and shivering, still coming. "I can't believe you."

"What?" Thane whispered, smoothing Gayle's hair, kissing her temple gently. "What, babe?"

"Everything," Gayle said with a sigh, boneless with pleasure. "You are so fucking talented, and so beautiful, and so...good."

"I guess you liked it, huh?" Thane chuckled, supremely satisfied.

"Nah, not really." Weakly, Gayle bit Thane's ear. "But I *would* like to try reenacting that shower scene."

"Now there's an idea."

"Is that by any chance what you had in mind when you let me read that?" Gayle met Thane's gaze and arched a brow. "Hmm?"

"Who, me?" Thane smiled, her eyes dancing. "No way. *I'm innocent.*"

PRIMAL PAS DE DEUX

BY RADCLYFFE AND KATLYN

The air hangs heavy with a mixture of smoke and sweat as I enter the club. My eyes sweep the room, taking in everything, everyone, yet settling on nothing and no one in particular. I move down the open stairs toward the bar hidden in a recess at the back of the room. Bodies are pressed tight against the once highly polished surface, which now shows signs of long years of faithful duty. Each scar on the dark wood is a proclamation of some former existence, an experience—a moment forever etched in the flesh of this place. I wonder if the scars *we* carry are as invisible as we think—hope—or if our fragile flesh reveals all we are and have been with a single look.

I think too damn much, I know, but that is what I do. I analyze, tear apart, and disassemble each element of most everything I encounter, until I can put it back together again in some semblance of order and understanding. I do that with everything—well, everything except my own life. For that, there is no understanding. I ease between the masses of people and raise my hand for the bartender, who tilts her head in recognition. One thing I have found in small clubs and bars is that being a regular gets you quick service. Tonight is no different as the woman sets an ice-cold mug of beer in front of me and then turns to answer other beckoning calls.

My throat burns as the cold liquid flows down in one long, hard swallow, then I turn to watch the gyrating bodies on the dance floor. A few participants appear to be long-term partners just enjoying a night out on the town. Others are in full tribal dress, displaying their availability for all to see. Leather and flesh abound for all potential partners to appraise and rank. The smoky haze hovering like a thunderhead emphasizes the electricity in the air as it reflects the strobe lights bouncing from body to body.

I've been watching you from my shadowed corner since the instant you walked in. There are a hundred other women in this hot, sex-scented space, but you're the only one I see. The air around you shimmers with heat, or perhaps it's merely a reflection off your leathers. Can you feel my eyes on you? You're early. You wanted to stay away, but you can't, can you? I like knowing that you couldn't, that you had to come looking for it. You look *good,* in your arrogant butch way and the leather pants you wear like skin. They make you look tough; you *are* tough. Do you hope they'll toughen your heart as well?

You cruise the room, a shark among the unsuspecting swimmers, hungry and dangerous. My clit gives a quick jerk inside my tight 501s, and that swift pulse makes the tip rub against the seam of my pants. I'm hard; I've been waiting, too, to be caught, devoured, swallowed down. The head presses out beyond the hood, fat and firm. My need leaves a wet spot inside the threadbare denim. The crowd is so close around me that, unnoticed, I cup my crotch and massage the ache, but my clit only gets stiffer with every squeeze. If I don't stop, I'll come just from looking at you. But fuck, it feels good. I can't wait any longer. Catching my clit in my fingers, giving myself one final tug, I push off from the wall and shoulder through the crowd.

My lips curl as I watch the synchronization of lust and leather, remembering a time when I was among the many hunters in the feeding frenzy. Never again; not after...Shaking my head, I drain the glass, turn back toward the bar in search of a refill, and continue to eye the dancers in the dirty mirror opposite me. The bartender places another drink in front of me and continues on her way. I can feel the heat boiling from within, a heat so powerful it makes me ache to succumb to its demanding call. I sip the beer from the frozen mug and watch as the delicate ice crystals on the rim melt instantly when I touch glass to my hot and hungry lips. The droplets slide down the surface of the glass, and I know that I am just as wet and slick. I suck in my bottom lip to catch a stray drop before it streaks down my chin and bite the tender flesh to quell the driving need within my belly. Then some unseen force takes control as I feel the heat of you against my back.

I slide my arms under your leather jacket, circle your waist and, ever so slowly, cup your breasts in the palms of my hands. You jerk infinitesimally, then stiffen as your iron control kicks in. I smile, my lips brushing the soft leather at your neck. I love to take you by surprise, love to tease you. There's nothing quite so sexy as a butch in need, unless it's two. You hide that need well, from everyone but me. And I know just how to break that pristine hold you exert on your power. There's a connection between your tits and your clit. Just feeling the stone-hard peaks beneath my fingers, knowing you're getting harder—*everywhere*—as I slowly squeeze, makes my nipples contract. I rub my breasts across your back to tease them. Now who's topping whom, huh, baby?

My hand trembles as you pinch my already erect nipples between your fingers, and I set the glass down hard. In a surreal moment I notice a new indentation in the scarred surface of the bar, marking another moment in time—a new experience etched into the flesh of this place. A smile teases my lips as my eyes trace the new mark, and I know this will be a moment I will not soon forget.

I attempt to turn around, but your body pressing against the length of my back holds me in place. Your breath is warm on my neck, and I shiver as your tongue traces the outline of my ear. I feel the wet heat flowing between my legs. The insistent throbbing of my clit, bound tightly in the skintight leather pants, makes my hips thrust forward involuntarily, and I release a quiet whimper that only you can hear.

You're teasing me, testing my resolve—my strength. The molten heat boils beneath the surface, and the urge to allow you to take control is powerful. My eyes, veiled and dark, meet yours in the mirror, and you smile. You think you have conquered me, and as I return the knowing smile, I instantly feel a renewed strength in your posture as you press your body closer to mine. But not tonight, not this night anyway. You're mine, and I will play you as I know you like it.

I don't expect your next move, but I should have. How many times have I bottomed for you? When you reach behind, grab my waistband, and pull my crotch into your ass, my clit bangs against the seam of my jeans again, and I almost fall down. Then you begin jerking up on my jeans, swift hard tugs, over and over, the material fisted in your strong hand. You're jerking me off with the ridge of denim squeezing down on the head of my clit. The pressure is making my stomach churn and my head light. Jesus, I want to come in my pants, right here and now. *Oh man, I really need to get off.* I forget about topping. It's not my nature where you're concerned. I push back, rotating my hips enough to flick my whole clit back and forth over the taut material. The shaft is so stiff it's almost enough—oh fuck, yeah, I'm almost there. Eyes nearly closed, I lower my forehead so it just touches the back of your head, still twisting your nipples as my clit dances on the edge. Silently intoning, *I'm gonna come for you, baby. Just a little more.*

I know you have nothing on beneath those 501s, and the thought of your clit pressing against the rough fabric almost makes me lose control. I ache to feel your hard clit between my fingers, feel your slick heat bathe my hand. The women on each side of us are facing away, and I know we are hidden from roaming eyes. My hand fumbles blindly with the buttons of your jeans until you subtly reach down and undo them for me. I can feel the heat radiating from you, and I delve deep within the tight confines of your jeans.

Oh thank Christ, you're going to touch me. I just have to try not to come all over your hand with the first contact. I might be a butch bottom, but I'm not submissive. But I am so ready to blow—

I'm not sure—oh man...My breath stops dead as you slide a finger on either side of my clit. When you start to stroke it, the pleasure floods my belly.

"Baby, you're making me come."

Did I say that out loud? I can't tell. I didn't mean to. I'm so hard, so swollen, and I can't keep from thrusting my hips into your palm. I pull on your nipples mercilessly as you tug on my clit. I'm gonna shoot in your hand...

I hold still, forcing you to ride my hand, making you work for what we both so desperately need. You're wet and hard as you pump your clit between my fingers. I know the chance of being found out makes the experience even more exciting for you, yet you move against my hand almost imperceptibly, trying not to draw attention from those around us. My shoulder is pressed against the back of the woman next to me, so I have to move slowly. I know, given the sexual electricity in this place, that we will be discovered if I am not careful. Yet I can feel your frustration as your body demands a quick resolution, and I give way to your begging eyes, locked on mine in the mirror.

Oh Jesus, *fuck* don't stop. I'm about to lose my load right here—*oh, please*—I start rocking a little harder...fuck if anyone can see me...I don't care, let 'em watch you jerk me off. The motion pushes and pulls my stone hard-on through your fingers. Oh yeah, yeah—that'll do it. You're gonna jerk me off right—

You slide into me, stalling the come for a second and driving me even higher. I moan out a hot breath against your neck, my body trembling against your back. You roll my clit under your thumb as you fill me up, fuck me deep. You're gonna make me come. Come so hard, come so deep—

You're stone hard as I roll your clit beneath my thumb. You jerk and clamp down tight around my fingers when I quickly flick the tip of my thumb across your clit. I know you're getting close, I can feel it, and I lick my lips imagining the taste of you against my tongue.

I can feel the pounding of your heart against my back as your thrusts quicken and become more demanding. Nonchalantly, I bring the glass to my mouth and drink, driving any suspicion away from your movement behind me as you draw closer to the release you seek. Casually, I look into the mirror and our eyes meet. My clit jerks in response to the desperate need etched upon your face, and I know that I could come just from watching your release. I know because I have before, many times, as you've teased me, driven me to release without ever touching me.

I find your eyes in the mirror—I want to see you see me come. I know when I go off on your fingers, in your hand, pumping against your ass, you'll almost come too—just from seeing my face the instant I come, pleasure and pain and...I'm coming baby, feel my clit get big, hard...I'm clamping down on your hand and I can't hold on and I'm screaming inside and it's everywheresogood...

I smile at your reflection and feel your clit swell even more just an instant before you explode. You bite the flesh of my neck to stifle the scream that rises from your throat as you come on a long, moaning sigh. I still my hand and feel your body tremble against me as you spasm around my fingers, drenching me with your come, and I watch your eyes dilate and become unfocused while you ride the wave of your orgasm.

Slowly, your body relaxes against me, and even before I remove my hand and turn around, I am aching to touch you again. I press my lips against your sweat-dampened forehead before leaning back against the bar and looking into your eyes. "Hey."

Your arms circle my waist, and your lips seek out the tender flesh of my neck before you answer.

"Hey, yourself." I give you my most innocent smile. "Fancy meeting you here."

Your fingers snake back under my jacket to pinch my aching nipples. "Yeah, well, I got an interesting message this afternoon suggesting that tonight might be a good time for me to visit the club." My body jerks as you slide your leg between mine and press hard against my swollen clit. My words are whispered and broken as a wave of desire and need burns deep within my belly. "And you know I'm always up for an adventure."

"Really?" I smile again.

"*Really.*"

"How was it?"

"Worth the wait."

"Good to hear." I should be wiped out, but once is never enough with you. I am still hard, still aching. I pull your hand between my thighs, press your fingers to the wet denim, pump on them a little.

"But I'm not done yet. You'd better have a cock inside those hot leather pants, because I want to lay you down on your back and take you inside. I want you to watch my face while you fuck me. I want you to watch my hands while I ride your cock and jerk off my clit and come all over your clit. You ready for another dance?"

I take your hand in mine, press it against the front of my leathers, and smile when your eyes widen with excitement at the feel of the hard bulge. "With you? Always."

OFF THE METER

It was ten minutes to one. Ten minutes until I was officially off the meter. I'd started work at eleven the previous day. That's eleven *a.m.* I'd lost count of the number of times I'd circumvented Manhattan, north-south, east-west, around and around. But I couldn't complain; I'd been busy all day and had a pocket full of neatly folded bills, my tips, to show for it. There was a lot of money to be made driving a cab in New York City, if you were faster and more fearless than the other cabbies. And I was.

Still, I was feeling the effects of the long hours of fighting the traffic, hyped on adrenaline, too much caffeine, and not enough food. I should've passed up the last fare, but there was something about the way she stood under the awning of the Waldorf-Astoria, clearly in need of a cab but too aloof and sophisticated to flag one down, that caught my eye. No unseemly show of waving arms and shouting in the streets for *her.* Despite the fact that I'd already lit the off-duty sign on my roof box, signaling that I was out of service, and was headed back to the barn, I swerved across three lanes of traffic and screeched to a halt in front of the slender redhead in the sleek black dress and stiletto heels.

When she didn't move, I thought at first that I'd been mistaken about her needs. Illuminated by the lights of the grand hotel's entrance, her face was elegantly made up. A diamond choker nestled in the hollow of her throat, and her eyes as they swept over me without the slightest sign of interest were remote. She looked more the type to be waiting for a limo than a yellow cab. Then, although she hadn't made the slightest movement, I suddenly knew exactly why she waited. Slamming the transmission into park, I bounded from the front seat, having totally forgotten that five minutes earlier I had been reeling with exhaustion and nerves, and hurried around the front of my vehicle.

"Taxi, madam?" Don't ask me why I said that. She just looked the part. Regal. Yes, that was it, as if the ordinary worlds of ordinary people revolved in some parallel universe from which she was far removed. I wished for a crimson-lined cape to spread over the littered sidewalk. Bowing slightly and feeling not the least bit foolish, I indicated the slightly battered vehicle with a sweep of my arm and an open hand, presenting it as if it were a gleaming coach with four white steeds.

She tilted her head and nodded with a faint smile. "Yes. Thank you."

Don't ask me either why I opened the *front* door and not the rear, or why she slid in without the slightest hesitation. But thirty seconds later I was settled behind the wheel, and she was only inches away, angled slightly to face me, her knees pressed demurely together and pulled partway up onto the seat.

"Where may I take you?" My throat was dry and my voice sounded unusually deep to my own ears. Carefully, I placed my hands at two and ten on the familiar wheel, its warm, smooth surface imprinted on my palms from years of intimacy. Suddenly self-conscious in my well-worn work khakis and white cotton T-shirt, I felt like a peasant in the presence of a noblewoman.

"Would you mind very much opening the windows?" Her voice was silky smooth and honey rich. "I dislike air-conditioning."

"It's too hot outside to do much for you," I replied as I dutifully lowered both front windows. The August night was thick and humid and immediately settled around us like fog.

"I find a breath of air on my skin refreshing, especially when it's warm."

I turned my head and met her eyes. They were large, long lashed, and deep, deep blue. Ocean-drowning blue. I never even considered not going under. "I forgot where you said you wanted to go."

She laughed, a surprisingly full and enormously sensuous sound. She leaned forward, her hand inches from my thigh, and flipped off the air-conditioning. "That's because I didn't tell you."

"Just say where." Now I understood how monarchies survived for centuries. Being the recipient of her smile was better than gold. *Allow me to serve you.*

"Take me for a ride."

My mind went completely blank, my stomach turned somersaults, and a ball of fire ignited between my thighs. *Command me, I'm yours.*

"How far..." My voice cracked and I cleared my throat. "How far did you have in mind?"

She rested her fingertips ever so gently on the top of my right hand, which was now clenched around the gearshift. "How much time do you have?"

The muscles in my forearm quivered uncontrollably as I nodded to the blank face of the rectangular fare box mounted to my dash. "I'm done for the day."

"Well then," she said, her fingers insinuating between mine, "it's up to you, isn't it?"

Carefully, fearful that I would dislodge her hand from mine, I maneuvered the gearshift into drive, flicked my eyes to the side-view mirror, and eased into the late-night traffic. "Your wish is my command, m'lady."

"You honor me," she murmured, sliding infinitesimally closer, leaving only a sliver of space between her thigh and mine. Her fingers left my hand and brushed with mesmerizing frequency up and down my bare arm. "Pretend I'm a tourist and show me the sights."

"Are you? A tourist?" I had no idea why it felt completely natural for the stranger to caress me. Her touch was gentle, but possessive. And it felt exactly right.

"In a way." She sighed quietly and rested her cheek against my shoulder, her breast gently cushioned against my upper arm.

I did the only thing I could. I took her on a slow tour of Manhattan, pointing out the sights as I drove: St. Patrick's Cathedral, the theater district, Times Square. Now and then she inclined her head to look up through the windshield or leaned forward to peer out the driver's window for a better view. Each small movement of her body against mine caused my heart to race and my nerves to jangle. Somehow, I kept my eyes on the streets even as my awareness dissolved into sensations of her. Her scent, delicate and mysterious, stirred my blood; her voice, a mellifluous murmur, sent chills down my spine; her body, firm and warm and enticing, aroused mine.

"There." I raised my free hand, the one where her fingers still rested on my wrist, and pointed briefly. "The Empire State Building."

"Mmm, very phallic." One hand drifted to my thigh as she caught my right hand in the other and drew it down to her lap, linking our fingers once again.

I laughed with surprise at the comment and pleasure at the unexpected touch on my leg. "Seems to be a theme with monuments. I guess it's all about the power."

"Too obvious," she murmured. She moved closer and rested the tip of her chin on the point of my shoulder. I felt her gaze hot against my cheek. "I prefer a subtler kind of power."

"And what would that be?" My voice was barely a whisper because I was finding it hard to move air in and out of my chest. Her palm rested on the inside of my leg, less than an inch from my crotch. I knew without looking that there was a damp spot soaked through the material stretched between my thighs, and if she touched me there even by accident, she would know without doubt what she had done to me.

"The kind that has nothing to do with winning and losing." She pressed her mouth to the side of my neck and traced the tip of her tongue over the pulse that beat frantically beneath my skin. "Passion is the true power." Her fingers danced up my fly to my stomach, where she tugged my T-shirt from my pants and slid her hand underneath. "*Shared* passion."

My stomach went rigid, my thighs stiffened, and I had to concentrate not to press down on the gas pedal and rocket us up Sixth Avenue. Her hand was so hot my skin burned. When she massaged me in slow circles, the pressure went straight into my clit. If my legs hadn't already been spread, I would have had to part them, just to make room for it as it promptly swelled and twitched. I groaned softly, and I swear she laughed.

"Take me through Central Park."

"You won't...see much at night."

"Mmm, I'm not thinking of the scenery *outside*."

As she spoke, she drew my hand beneath the hem of her dress. While she leaned against me, still stroking my stomach, she guided the backs of my fingers up and down the inside of her thigh. When I felt the subtle lift of her hips beside me, I knew I was lost.

"I can't drive like this," I whispered.

"Find a place to pull over." The hint of command was still in her voice, but the faint tremor there now went right to my head.

My vision blurred for an instant and reflections from neighboring headlights became dancing moonbeams. I struggled to keep the cab in the lane. "Oh God—"

"Steady. There's time."

I drew a tremulous breath and squeezed down hard on the steering wheel with my left hand, blinking to clear my eyes. "I can't...I can't think. I want to touch you so much."

Her laughter held a note of triumph. "Will that help your concentration?"

To emphasize her point, she brushed my fingers higher between her thighs, the silk of her dress sliding up my arm as my fingertips slid over silken skin. I touched slick wet heat and gave a sharp cry of shock.

"No," she murmured throatily, "I didn't think so."

Mercifully, I'd just reached the entrance to the park where the traffic at least would be thinner. I made the mistake of glancing down into her lap and saw our arms disappearing beneath the silvery blackness of her dress, even as my fingers beneath it parted her ready flesh. I veered into a tiny turnaround and with my left hand awkwardly jammed the transmission into park while in the same motion turning toward her. In less than a second my mouth was against her ear, my fingers spread over the cleft between her thighs, cupping all of her, hot and wet and swollen. "I can't wait. Please, may I touch you?"

"Yes," she breathed, "I give you leave."

Abruptly, she released her hold on my hand where she held it between her legs and pushed both of hers beneath my T-shirt to grasp my bare breasts. The force of her fingers closing on my tense nipples and swollen breasts wrenched another cry from my throat. Before the sound died, her mouth was on my neck, the weight of her body forcing me back against the seat.

Even as her lips and teeth and mouth nipped at my skin, I fumbled with my left hand between the seat and the door, found the seat release lever, and pulled it. The front seat slid back away from the steering wheel, enough at least to allow us to turn and face each other. I arched my neck, offering myself, as she sucked on the tender flesh just below my jaw. Gently, I eased my fingers into her depths, marveling at the heat and softness. She moaned and pressed down against my hand.

"We can't—" My body bowed from the seat as she lowered her head and caught a nipple in her teeth through my T-shirt. Tugging at it, making the blood roar in my head, she adroitly opened the button on my chinos and flicked down the zipper. "Police...could come."

"They won't," she said fiercely, rolling her hips in my palm. "Come deeper inside me. Fill me up, make me come."

I gazed down through clouded eyes and saw her push her hand down my pants. The sight alone nearly made me come. I knew as soon as she touched me I would explode, and I wanted her to come first. Her fingers glided through the dampness between my legs just as I entered her. As I filled her, holding her in my palm, I worked my thumb back and forth over her clitoris. The muscles spasming around my fingers signaled she was nearing her climax.

"That's right," she murmured, "that's right. I'm coming."

Her fingers closed around my clitoris as the first wave of her orgasm rolled through her. She pressed her face to my breasts, rocked her hips convulsively against my hand and arm, and even though she shuddered and moaned, still managed to jerk me to a shattering climax.

For minutes, possibly hours, I was blind and deaf and barely breathing. The engine idled quietly in the background, a soothing contrast to our hoarse cries and desperate moans. When at last I fell back against the seat, limp and thoroughly sated, she raised her head and kissed the corner of my mouth.

"Wherever this spot is, it should get four stars in the guidebook."

"It's not on my usual tour route," I rejoined lazily.

She caught my wrist as I was about to slip out of her and held my fingers inside, undulating her hips slowly. "No, not yet. You feel so good filling me."

"We have to get moving." My neck muscles were so weak I wasn't sure I would be able to sit up, but I managed to turn my head on the seat. Her eyes as they held mine were liquid, so dark and satisfied they appeared black. "We haven't finished our tour."

The corner of her mouth lifted and she squeezed down around my fingers one more time before gently guiding me out. "You mean there's more?"

"Uh-huh. Lots."

"Do you have time?"

"All the time in the world." I smiled and leaned forward to kiss her. "I'm off the meter, remember?"

OASIS

I'd worked all night—an emergency call-out. By the time I stumbled in just after dawn, she was already up. I muttered hello; she gave me a sympathetic smile. Then I showered to wash away the lingering scent of stress and sweat and fell into bed. When I awoke, it was late in the day—one of those still, sultry summer afternoons. I'd kicked off the sheet and lay on my stomach, naked. The air was heavy and hot in the bedroom, despite the open windows, and the desultory breeze carried teasing hints of barbeque, laughter, and simple pleasures long forgotten. As I floated on the cusp of sleep and awareness, I had the sense of being very old, or very young—and I ached to drift forever in that timeless womb where life was safe and easy.

The house was silent, but I knew she was in her shop working. If I lay very still and concentrated, I could just make out the distant sound of a phonograph. Not a stereo, but an old-fashioned record player with a tone arm and a diamond-tipped needle playing 45s from an era long past. Patsy Cline, walking after midnight and crying over sweet dreams of faded love. We had that in common, she and I—that melancholy even in the midst of happiness.

I shifted onto my back and the tiny breath of air from the window skimmed across my breasts, my belly. Stretching lazily, I brushed a hand over my stomach. Eyes closed, I could see her, bent over her worktable, absorbed in her latest project, humming unconsciously to the anthems of heartbreak and loss as her swift, sure hands manipulated a tiny tool and her laser-sharp blue eyes focused intently. I'd felt those eyes scorch my skin, those hands ignite my flesh. I knew what power, what passion, she conjured with a look, with a touch, when I lay beneath her.

My clitoris was suddenly hard.

The first tiny pulse of pleasure, the tingling rush of electricity, grew steadily more insistent until it was all I felt. Legs tensing, twisting slightly amidst the crumpled cotton sheets, I brushed my fingertips through the triangle of soft hair at the base of my belly. I could call her to me now, and she would come willingly. I could tell her of my needs, and she would answer them gladly. I could whisper my secret desires, and she would honor them reverently. And if I asked for nothing more than her hot mouth and her clever fingers to assuage my hunger, she would toss me that lazy grin and settle between my thighs and give herself to my pleasure.

I *could* call her to me, and knowing that truth was enough to make me leave her to her private contentment, for the moment.

But my body had stirred, and the need rode hard now between my thighs. It was the perfect setting for a slow, easy climb to satisfaction—sunlight dappled my skin in soft warm patches, a faint mist of sweat dampened my skin, and the languid swelling of desire thudded in the pit of my stomach. I lifted my hips, cupped a hand between my legs. As I caressed swollen, sensitive lips—ever so lightly—my clitoris, still hidden, twitched. A quiet moan drifted away on the air.

I dipped a fingertip into the satiny moisture and deliberately coated the length of my clitoris. The feather-light touch, all I allowed myself, sent pleasure rippling through my belly. My legs stiffened, and I sighed. I knew this song—sweet dreams of you...

So good.

Slowly, I stroked and circled and pressed until the clench of muscles deep inside, the sweet ache of blood rushing into tender tissues, the steady beat of desire that kept time with my heart brought another cry from my throat.

Oh God.

My hips rose and fell with each long, smooth glide of my fingers. I struggled to prolong the wanting, forcing my hand to still when the pressure built too high, even though my body screamed for me to drive myself fast and hard to orgasm. Then a rush of passion flooded my hand, and the first flutter of release whispered along my inner thighs. I bit down on my lip, a futile effort to hold back the tide.

Oh, not yet.

Carefully, I grasped my stiff clitoris between thumb and forefinger and squeezed, temporarily forestalling my climax. But I couldn't help but pump my hips as I cupped my sex. The control I prided myself on was slipping.

Close. Close now.

I whimpered brokenly, needing desperately to let go. If I just rubbed the hea—

"Please wait."

The gentle plea pierced the roaring in my head, and I struggled to open my eyes. Turning my head, I saw her leaning in the doorway across from the bed, her eyes on me, her hand moving slowly beneath her gray cotton T-shirt, fingers tugging at the hard ball of her nipple.

"Hi," I said, my voice husky with lust. I stopped the motion of my hand, but my fingers still trembled against my wet, pulsating flesh. "Finished...work?"

Her smile was lopsided, her eyes heavy lidded as her gaze drifted down my body and lingered on my hand. "Yeah—did you finish yours?"

I rolled my hips, the pressure on my distended clitoris making me gasp. "Almost."

"Want company, or should I just watch?"

I heard the hunger in her voice and knew that the flush of sex on my neck and breasts signaled how near I was to coming. I knew what she wanted, and I knew that she would do whatever I asked. Smiling, I drew my damp, shining fingers up the center of my abdomen and circled a nipple, leaving the hard nub glistening.

"Jesus," she whispered reverently.

"Your choice...but tell me soon. I need to come really bad."

"Turn over," she said sharply, pushing away from the wall. "And *don't* touch yourself again unless I tell you to."

Rolling onto my stomach and closing my eyes, I cradled my head in my arms. I could smell my arousal and knew she would, too. My clitoris beat a frantic rhythm between my thighs. "I'm going to come right away. As soon as you touch me."

"No," she said from somewhere behind me. "You're not."

All of my senses were heightened. The sound of a drawer opening cracked like thunder, the snick of a zipper sliding down sliced through me like a knife. The snap of a buckle struck my depths like a fist. I ached to come. When her weight settled carefully onto the foot of the bed, I very slowly pulled one knee up toward my chest, letting her see the rosy dew of my excitement. Then I waited, poised to explode.

She moved slowly, carefully, between my legs. When she touched my swollen inner lips, I jumped, uttering a soft moan.

"You're so wet," she murmured, painting the sensitive folds and valleys of my sex with a fingertip dipped in my own desire. She drew the wetness to my anus and circled the opening. The tiny muscle contracted, and I felt the pressure straight through to my clit.

"You'll make me come," I gasped.

"Shh. I won't."

She lingered for a moment as I lifted my hips, supplicant and silent. I moaned when she moved away, denying me, then sighed as her fingers slid forward, teased my clit for a tantalizing instant, then glided between my labia. Slowly, she entered, stretching me gently, moving her fingers in and out a fraction of an inch at a time. The tension pulled the hood tight around my clit. *Oh, yes.* Wanting more, I pushed back and forth between her hand behind and the bed below.

"Stop that," she warned, a hint of laughter in her voice.

"Feels so good...touch my clit, honey. Please."

"Maybe," she whispered, deep inside me now, "if you're good."

She shifted closer, up on her knees, withdrawing her fingers to circle my clit for just one final second—teasing me, making me cry out. She knew how much I loved to have her rub her fingers over my wet clit.

"Make me come," I begged.

"Like this?" She pressed harder and my whole body jerked.

"Oh yeah." The roaring in my head was back. I couldn't breathe. She brought me almost to the edge, then stopped. I collapsed, gasping. "Please...I'm almost there."

"Mmm. I know." She cupped my hips with both hands and lifted. "Get up on your knees."

Trembling, I obeyed. I pressed my face to my bent arms, supporting myself, and waited. *Hurry. Oh God, hurry.*

The head of her cock slid between my wet lips, back to front, rubbing the undersurface of my exposed clitoris. The pressure made me want to come instantly.

"I can't take that," I gasped.

"Jesus, neither can I."

Her breathing grew harsher, faster. The hand she kept on my back to guide me trembled. I knew the cock was pressing against her clit as she steadied it in the harness with her hand. As she teased me with it, she teased herself. I wanted to make her need to come the way she made me. Aching, begging for it. I thrust back against her cock and pushed it hard into her crotch.

She groaned and worked the head inside me. My clit twitched, grew larger. She rocked her hips, carefully. She was so careful with her cock. I didn't want her careful. I wanted her inside. I wanted her to come inside me. I wanted to come. My clit was so hard now, I had to touch it. I started to slide a hand under my belly, but she stopped me.

"Not until I come."

"I can't wait. I can't."

Wordlessly, she pushed all the way in, her belly against my butt now, the cock filling me. Finally, she reached around with one hand and found my clit. When she pulled it gently, I screamed.

My words came out a plea, a litany of supplication. "I want to come. Please, can I come. Please, honey..."

She was moaning softly, working her cock in and out, faster and faster—enough for her to jerk off her clit, but not enough to hurt me. Her fingers slid up and down the shaft of my clitoris, then rolled over the tip.

"I'm gonna come soon," she whispered unevenly, her damp forehead pressed to my shoulder. "You ready?"

"God, *yes.*"

I bucked on her cock and ground against her fingers the way I needed to come. The more I moved, the more the cock worked her clit. Her hips pumped wildly now, her teeth bruising the skin at the back of my shoulder. We were both moaning.

"I'm coming," I cried, humping her hand as her hips beat against my ass. As my clit exploded, she cried out, pushed her cock all the way inside me, and came on it.

I collapsed, shuddering, onto the bed. Even as she jerked with the last spasms of her orgasm, she was careful not to hurt me. She eased down on my back, still inside me.

"Glad I happened by," she murmured contentedly, her hands curled around my forearms, her cheek to my neck.

I sighed, still contracting around her cock, the final waves of pleasure spreading through me like warm sunlight. Outside the window life went on, but here, there was only us. "Me too, honey. Me too."

ONLY A WORD AWAY

The rookie officer sat at a crowded desk in a cramped corner of the station house, her back to the room, her surprisingly delicate, long-fingered hands moving gracefully over the keyboard. With her head tilted to one side as she studied the computer monitor, her red-gold hair—cropped close at the back of her neck and cut slightly longer on the top and sides—fell onto her forehead in a careless wave.

"Yo, Reynolds. You 'bout done with those reports?"

Tap, tap.

"If you get it done before six, we can catch a beer with the rest of the guys from the day shift," her training officer, an ex-football player who still looked the part, called from across the room in an aggrieved tone. "Jesus, if I'd known it was going to take you this long to finish the paperwork..." He fell silent, as if suddenly realizing that the only alternative would be to do it himself, and that was a far from satisfactory choice. After all, what were rookie partners for?

"Reynolds?"

Tap, tap. Tap, tap, tap...tap.

"Man, you can really type." His tone was reverent as he shoved himself up from the desk where he had parked his butt to talk over the events of the day with his buddies. As he wended his way between chairs abandoned haphazardly and desks angled askew, he asked, "How much longer, Rey?"

Reynolds jumped as the deep male voice, close by now, finally penetrated her consciousness. Heart racing, she rocketed the cursor arrow to the minimize box.

Click.

The ever-so-tasteful Miss July *Penthouse* centerfold screensaver appeared. The uplifted, rose-tipped breasts and airbrushed hint of down at the cleft between the full voluptuous thighs didn't even register in Reynolds's mind. Closing her fists to hide the faint trembling in her hands, she snapped, "What?"

"Hey!" Her partner's eyebrows rose at the unusual edge in her voice, and he held up both hands as if to ward off an oncoming vehicle. "I just wanted to know when you would be done. We're all gonna go out for a beer."

"I still got the 10-55 from over on Sansom to write up. And then the 10-16." Drunk drivers and domestic disturbances, the staple of patrol officers' days. "Did you get the husband booked?"

"Yep. Just finished."

"It's gonna take me at least another hour with his paperwork."

"Well, hell." He actually sounded disappointed. "What about leaving it for tomorrow morning?"

Reynolds shook her head. "Go without me. If we get busy at start of shift tomorrow, we'll be late filing these reports. Then we'll never hear the end of it from the sarge."

"You sure?"

"Yes." The words came out fast and hard. "Jesus, just *go* already."

"Okay, okay. I'm gone. Thanks." He slapped her affectionately on the back before turning away.

Immediately, Reynolds brought the dialogue box back up and stared at the last words, wondering—not for the first time—just what she was getting into.

BLUE: I miss you when we can't
       connect.

She directed the cursor to the prominent X in the upper right-hand corner of the screen. Just a flick of her finger, and it would all be gone. The questions, the uncertainties—the excitement. That free-fall feeling in the pit of her stomach when the screen lit up and the characters started to dance across her field of vision.

She released the mouse and put her fingers on the keys.

Rydl: I'm back...you still there?

The ensuing "silence" echoed the hollow feeling in the pit of her stomach as her emotions warred.

She's gone.

And that was just as well. They'd almost reached the point of no return—neither had acknowledged it, but Reynolds could feel it. Her entire day, *every* day, had become centered on those few times when she could slip away and log on—sneaking a minute after roll call, five minutes away from filling out reports, another couple when she was supposed to be checking one of the convoluted databases for outstanding warrants. Precious stolen moments in which to search for the familiar icon, those four bold letters.

BLUE: thought I'd lost you

No, it would be so easy for me to disappear, but I can't stay away from you.

Rydl: sorry, public place

BLUE: you off work soon?

Rydl: about an hour

BLUE: meet me here 10 pm?? Alone?

Reynolds hesitated for just a second, then typed: **Yes**

Sitting in the dark in her den at 10:05 p.m., the dim glow of the monitor the only illumination, Reynolds stared at the screen. She pressed her hands to her bare thighs, fingers twitching.

BLUE: Ryd?

BLUE: Are you there?

BLUE: R? Honey?

Honey. She closed her eyes, took a breath, and tried to chase the butterflies from her stomach. Then, with careful deliberation, she replied.

Rydl: I'm here. But I can't stay.

I don't even know how I got this far. I don't want this.

BLUE: company?

No. I'm terrified. I want...God, I want...

Reynolds logged off, then sat with her gaze riveted to the blank screen, breathing as heavily as if she'd just finished a five-mile run. Aching. Instantly lonely.

Jesus. I can't just leave her out there with no explanation, can I? Oh, why the hell not, Rey? You don't even know her!

Except that wasn't exactly true—in fact, it was very far from true. They'd met only weeks before, but it seemed like months. It started simply enough—she stumbled into one of those chat rooms on the Net for women in law enforcement. It was ostensibly a place to network and discuss career strategies, but it turned out to be a safe haven where women who were often isolated at work could find support from others with like experiences. It was about connecting and community. It was about not being alone, when so very few people in her life—even her family and friends—really understood why she had chosen to do what she was doing. It was difficult to share her fears and doubts and disappointment when those she turned to only urged her to walk away. So, when she found these women, she sensed a kinship that she had experienced nowhere else in her life.

She just lurked for a while at first, getting a feel for the people, the topics, the back-and-forth of the discussions. It was amazing how quickly she came to recognize the various individuals, each with her own unique style. Not just different opinions, but different temperaments, senses of humor, and personalities—some aggressive, some calm and rational, some sarcastic. Before long she found herself looking for a particular participant to sign on. BLUE was funny and bright, and they seemed to share many similar views. During a particularly involved discussion of the pros and cons of mixed-gender teams on the job, they'd left the chat room to instant message. They'd IM'd for hours. Soon they were e-mailing first thing in the morning and on lunch breaks and chatting privately every night. Neither of them asked the other's real-life name; neither of them offered it. They were who they were, right there in black and white and all the nuances in between.

So why are you running away? But she knew why. Had known even before BLUE had said...what she said. *She took a chance. She told you the truth. And this is what you do?*

Reynolds's stomach clenched. *Oh, God. What if I've hurt her? What if she's really gone?*

Her hands flew to the keyboard and she logged back on. *Come on. Come on.*

```
Rydl: BLUE? BLUE? Are you th
BLUE: I'm here What happened?
Rydl: I'm sorry...I logged off
BLUE: Why? Are you angry with me?
```

```
Rydl: No. Of course not.
BLUE: If it's because of what I said
      earlier—
Rydl: No.
```

But it was, wasn't it? Had she really been that surprised when BLUE had confessed to being attracted to her—after they had been writing two or three times a day, *for weeks?* Sharing things she hadn't told another soul? Carefully probing. *What kind of things do you like to do outside of work? What kind of movies? Books? Are you single?*

And then BLUE had asked the question. *Have you ever had sex online?* And said what she'd said. *Because I'd like to...with you.*

Reynolds shook her head. *That's crazy. Just because I...like her...doesn't mean it's something sexual. Just because I look for her e-mail first thing in the morning, before I even make coffee...*

She laughed out loud, a shaky laugh that sounded weak to her own ears. Just as her rationalizations rang with the hollow notes of self-deception.

And I check for mail from her every few hours—and I'm terribly disappointed when there's none there. And she makes me laugh, and she makes me want to tell her things about myself from when I was ten years old, for Christ's sake.

She didn't know what to say. Yes, I feel what you feel? Was that even possible with someone she'd never met?

```
BLUE: It's okay, you know. I won't
      touch you if you don't want me to
      <g>
Rydl: I didn't say that.
```

FUCK! What are you doing! You can't seriously be considering this! Of course not. You're a professional, a police officer—people like you don't do this—do they? She willed her hands not to move onto the keyboard.

```
BLUE: i won't even touch myself if
      you tell me not to <vbg>
```

Reynolds closed her eyes, trying not to imagine it. Trying desperately to ignore the immediate flood of heat between her thighs. Her hands moved on their own.

```
Rydl: Are you?
BLUE: yes is that all right?
```

Reynolds swallowed. Stared at the words. Envisioned the woman reading the phrases that connected them physically, as surely as if they were in the same room. Her fingers began to tremble. What was worse, she felt a trickle of wetness as the throbbing escalated between her legs.

```
Rydl: Is it what you want?
BLUE: oh yes. I want you to feel me
Rydl: Are you wet?
BLUE: mmm, all day. are you
Rydl: Yes.
```

Jesus, Rey, get a grip! She was mesmerized by the voice she could almost hear. She shifted on the seat, her thighs inside loose silk boxers tightly closed. *I'll just tell her to stop.*

```
BLUE: should I tell you?
Rydl: PLease
```

She waited, not thinking, her pulse racing.

```
BLUE: i've been thinking about you
      all day—my clit has been hard
      since i logged on—i'm stroking it
      now—lightly
Rydl: Where. tell me how you touch
      yourself
BLUE: just up and down the sides i
      can't press too hard—I'm afraid
      i'll come—i want to feel you first
      before i com,e—oh its so goodoh
Rydl: wait Blue wait
BLUE: sorry—godI amost came rgfht
      away—sorry
Rydl: let me do it
BLUE: oh yeahplease I want oyu to
      touch me so much
Rydl: tell me what you like
```

Reynolds slipped her fingers beneath her T-shirt. She found a nipple, brushed it lightly, then squeezed. Biting her lip, she moaned softly.

```
BLUE: stroke my clit - between your
      fingers up and don like thatoh yes
      like that
Rydl: Is it good? Is that what you
```

need?

BLUE: oh my god, yess—Ilove your
       fingers, touching me—rolling my
       clit -- god—I have to -stopp—ytoo
       close—

Reynolds closed her eyes, willing away the feel of that hard, wet clit between her fingers, the soft sighs of pleasure, the slight lift of hips into her palm. She tried too to ignore the surging rush of blood into her own aching sex.

Rydl: you feel so goodbaby
BLUE: letme - let me calmdow
Rydl: okay?
BLUE: lol ohyeah i want you to come
       with me-may i touch you
Rydl: PLease

It's just words—nothing's going to happen. Reynolds eased down in the chair, her eyes glued to the screen, her breathing sharp and quick. Without thinking, drawn by the steady pulse of pleasure between her legs, she ran the fingers of her left hand lightly up the inside of her thigh. When she reached the wide leg opening in her boxers and encountered the first trace of arousal dampening her skin, she stopped. That was all—no more. Words formed on the screen, a whisper in her ear.

BLUE: ohh, you are wet. and so
       swollen, so har dlaready god,
       youre beautiful. i have my fingers
       on your clit, softly—I want to
       feel you get hard for me

Reynolds's clit twitched, and she gasped in surprise. She moved her hand higher, into the moist curls between her legs, easing her lips apart. Oh, Christ. She *was* hard, and so goddamned wet. She stroked between her lips lightly for an instant, then pulled away as a shiver ran down her thighs.

BLUE: is it good right there? where
       i' touchig you baby, is it good?
Rydl: godyes
BLUE: i feel you shaking. i'm just
       going to rub you, one finger on
       each side of your clit—youre so
       warm—theres no hurry—

She was swelling, throbbing steadily. Now that she'd touched herself once, she was dying to continue. *Enough. Jesus...*

Rydl: this is making me crazy—

She typed with one hand, but she still wouldn't give in. The hand in her lap ached to reach for her clit—she pushed back in the chair, trying to ease the insistent pressure pounding in her belly.

BLUE: i'm sliding one finger inside of
you now, my thumb on your clit,
holding you, pressing higher—oh
god—let me feel youcome

For a second, Reynolds's vision dimmed as the muscles in her pelvis contracted. She wanted to be filled, needed *something* to relieve the relentless buildup of blood into the overstimulated nerve endings. She found her clit, pulled back the hood with her thumb and middle finger and flicked across the exposed tip with her index finger, the way she did when she wanted to come. She tugged the sensitive shaft, and her hips jerked. Nearly blind, she fumbled for the keys.

Rydl: ohh blu..i want t come

BLUE: i knowbaby...three fingers now,
my arm curving between your legs,
pumping hard...

Her feet dug into the carpet and her legs stiffened, almost painfully tight. Her hand was a blur, her fingers working her engorged clit from side to side, dipping down into her own wetness, pulling the thick warm come over the top, around the sides—

Rydl: ohh—its too good—gonna comme

BLUE: hold on—notyet—I'm deep
insidenow

Rydl: i'm—close—

BLUE: you're squeezing down onmy
fingers, gushing into my hand—my
teeth find your nipple—biting—

Rydl: dont stop—

Reynolds's right hand flew from the keys, joining the left between her legs, fingers driving inside; she was riding them now as she rode the thin edge of orgasm. Wildly, her eyes searched the screen—needing the final stroke. *Oh, fuck—so close—gotta come now—*

Rydl: plesecoming

Give me the words. Please-God-just-one-word—
BLUE: fuckingyou...drivingharder-now—
 faster—ohyeah—it's starting—

Reynolds fixed on the words, keening as the first beat of orgasm struck in the pit of her stomach—her head thrashing against the chair back, pelvis jerking erratically as she met the internal contractions with thrusts of her hand. She pressed down hard on her distended clit, forcing out every last explosive tremor. The words streaked the screen like tears as her cries trailed off to faint whimpers. *Oh so good...*

BLUE: you okay?

Reynolds tried to make her fingers function.

Rydl: demolished
BLUE: i'm a little wasted myself –
 god, you're fantastic-- <G>
Rydl: are you—did you—god, did you
 come?
BLUE: LOL Yeah when you did—I could
 tell and I-uh- Iwent off like
 arocket

Reynolds smiled, oddly pleased.

Rydl: Good.
BLUE: See you again?

Reynolds read the simple question over and over, searching for the right words. Then, very deliberately, she typed:

Tomorrow -- 10pm

BEYOND THE PALE

Iknew she'd come home tired. Actually, not merely tired—stressed, worn out, and just plain sick of the ruthless corporate arena she'd chosen as her battleground. She was good at it, buying and selling and controlling. I'm sure more than one competitor had called her a coldhearted bitch bull dyke while he'd watched his own meager "assets" shrivel and shrink away. She looked like the headhunter that she was—hard bodied and hard eyed and strong. She'd come home wired and unable to sleep. She'd come home needing to be held, and more, but I knew that she wouldn't ask.

Admitting that she needed me wasn't easy for her. Not just admitting it to *me*, but to herself. *I* knew that she did, and I knew that she knew it. But it was something that we rarely talked about. Now, needing isn't weakness, and I believe that somewhere in her heart, she believes that, too. But she is who she is, and if ever there was a woman tailored for the word *butch*, it's her.

So, when I give her what she can't ask for, I know what it means to be more than just needed. I know what it means to be essential. And that's why, when my friends sometimes look at me in confusion and ask, "How can you put up with her tough act all the time?" I just smile. I know who I am, and I know who she is. And most importantly, I know who we are together.

And when she came through the front door that night, I knew that I'd been right again. Briefcase in one hand, suitcase in the other, and dark smudges beneath her bone-weary charcoal eyes, she mustered up one of her swaggering grins and said, "Hi, baby. Your stud is home."

"Come upstairs, stud," I said, just before giving her a long deep kiss and a full body press. She felt good against me, solid and strong. All it took was the brush of her belt buckle pressing into my belly through my thin silk T-shirt to stir me up. Ignoring the flutter in the pit of my stomach and the rush of excitement, I took her hand and coaxed her toward the stairs. "Let's go get comfortable, and you can tell me all about your trip."

Once inside the bedroom, I brushed my palms over her chest and under the edge of her jacket, pushing it off her shoulders. "Stop that," I said admonishingly when she brushed her thumbs over my nipples. I'd missed her, and that first caress streaked through me like lightning, but I didn't let her see what it did to me. Struggling to keep my voice steady, I frowned. "You look like you slept in this suit."

She growled and slid her hand beneath my T-shirt. I pivoted away, taking her jacket with me. "This is going directly to the cleaners," I announced as I tossed it onto a chair. Then I stepped behind her and wrapped my arms around her waist, pressing close to her back. I was safer if she couldn't touch me, because she was so good at taking control. With my cheek against her shoulder blade, I one-handed the buttons on her shirt until it fell open, then tugged it and the thin tee beneath it from her pants. Deliberately, I allowed my fingers to drift over her breasts as I liberated them. She stiffened against me, but in typical fashion, made no sound. I often wonder if she really believes that I don't know how much she likes my touch. Then, with one hand pressed to her stomach, which was already tight the way it gets when she's excited, I opened her belt buckle with the other and pulled the length of leather from her trousers. As it thudded to the floor, I unbuttoned her fly and slid down the zipper. I didn't play with her as I often did, although I was dying to skim my fingers inside and tease her through that last thin barrier. If I made her too hot, too fast, she'd turn the tables on me. When she's dying to come, that's when she wants me most. "These too."

"What?"

Her voice was husky and low, and she sounded just a little confused.

"Your pants—to the cleaners. Step out of them." As I spoke, I hooked my thumbs inside the waistband, catching her underwear too, and pushed down. At the same time, she tried to get a hand between us to cup me, but I pressed tighter to her butt, preventing her from slipping her fingers between my legs. I was wet, and if she discovered it, she wouldn't stop touching me until I came. "It's late, baby. I'm tired."

"You think you can meet me at the door in nothing but that skimpy shirt and panties and I'm not going to touch you?"

She had that dangerous, edgy tone to her voice that said she didn't like to be denied. I had about two minutes before she was on top of me, and I wouldn't be able to say no. It had been a long week, and nothing made me come like her hands. I'd been ready for her for days. But she kicked out of the rest of her clothes and let me lead her by the hand to the bed.

"Come lie down, baby." I reached down, grasped the bottom of my silk tee, and stretched my arms above my head as I slowly drew it off, leaving only the white silk bikinis to cover me. Once again, I evaded her hands as I pulled back the crisp, fresh sheets and slipped into bed.

She came into my arms like I was her last refuge, pulling me to her, one arm encircling my waist, fitting every curve of her body to mine. I tucked my head into the shelter of her neck and kissed the undersurface of her jaw. "I've missed going to sleep with you."

"Yeah?"

She skimmed her fingers up my stomach and over my right nipple, catching my breast in the swell of her palm and squeezing gently. Both nipples stood up straight from the attention, and my clit did a little dance. I wanted her to keep touching me. I always did. I wanted to rock my hips against the thigh that she edged between mine. I wanted her soft skin rubbing over my hard clitoris. I could come that way, and she loved it. She loved it when I trembled and whimpered and couldn't hold back, pushing myself up and down her leg until I shattered.

That's what I wanted, but I knew it wasn't what she needed. I let her push her leg a little tighter against me, because then I could get mine between hers. I ignored the ache between my legs, the tiny whispers of need pulsing through me, as I rolled a little bit more on top of her, bringing just a little more of my weight between her thighs. The damp silk between us saved me, because I so wanted to come and the heat of her skin on my bare clit would have broken me.

"So, were you brilliant this week?" I asked casually as I stroked my fingers along the side of her breast.

"Uh-huh," she acknowledged lazily as she cupped my butt with both hands and pulled me hard against her.

I rubbed my thumb back and forth over her stiffening nipple, and when I heard her quick intake of breath, I bent my head and licked it. Then I eased away just enough to smooth my other hand up the inside of her thigh. Soon I alternated between teasing her breast and nipple with my lips and stroking the soft skin high up on her thigh with echoing circular caresses.

"Did you close the deal?" I asked softly.

"Mmm. Course."

When she lifted her hips and pushed down, the backs of my fingers brushed between her legs. Oh God, she was wet, so wet. I felt her slick come against my skin, and my insides tightened. I was already painfully swollen, my clit trembled madly, and I was so close to letting go. But this was for her. I turned on my side so we were face to face and some of the pressure eased enough for me to breathe.

"So tell me...about the meeting." Relaxed. Interested.

While she talked, something about mergers and margins and options, I made appreciative sounds while tracing patterns on her belly, down her thighs, and up the inside of her leg. Every now and then, I allowed my fingers to stray down into the cleft between her cheeks. When I did, her words hitched and stumbled. By the time I sucked her nipple into my mouth, she'd stopped talking. When I worked it between my lips, alternately tugging and tonguing it, she moaned softly. I flicked it a little harder, then bit lightly.

"Jesus," she groaned and reached between my legs, hooking a finger around my bikinis. "Take these off."

I drew my hips back and looked into her eyes. They were hazy and soft. *Almost.* With a single finger, I stroked between her labia to a spot just below her clitoris. And pressed. Her lids fluttered and she arched her neck. *There.*

"No," I murmured against her mouth, "not yet."

"I *want* you," she protested softly, but she caught her lip between her teeth and moaned when I slowly squeezed her clitoris.

"Please," I whispered, circling her with my fingertips now, "I want to taste you." She was so hard, I ached to get her into my mouth.

"Just...for a second."

I smiled. *Now.* I slid down the bed, between her legs, then glanced up to find her propped up on her elbows, watching me from beneath heavy lids. Her scent was rich, enticing, exciting. Our eyes locked, and I held her gaze as I stretched out my tongue, licked the edges of her lips, then went lower, circling the taut muscle. Her eyes widened, and her breathing got faster. I pressed one palm against her stomach. It was like a board. I licked her slowly, using the whole surface of my tongue, lapping at her, drinking her in. Her eyes were nearly closed, but still she tried to watch me as I teased her.

"I want to come now," she said quietly, almost calmly. When she sounded like that, I knew she was struggling not to explode. Not to scream.

"I want to lick you a little longer."

She choked back a whimper, her hands tangling in my hair as she tried to guide my mouth to her red, swollen clit. Her legs were trembling, her fingers fluttering in my hair. I knew she was close and that if I sucked her for very much longer she would come.

"Please."

I didn't want her to beg. I wanted to give her everything.

I sucked on her clit, pulled it in and out of my mouth, running my tongue back and forth over the tip. When her hips started to rock, I slipped two fingers inside her. I needed her to open for me. I used my tongue to push under the hood, bearing down on the most sensitive part of her clitoris. Her legs twisted, and she pushed hard against my face.

"I want to come. Please make me come."

Three fingers now, my thumb and small finger curled into my palm. I could make her come with my mouth now—I *would* make her come if I kept up the attention to her clit. But I wanted more, and she needed more.

She held my head in both hands, pressing against me, her belly tight, quivering. "Come on, baby. Come on. God, make me come."

I lifted my lips away, raised up on my knees between her legs, and angled my arm slightly—four fingers. My head was spinning, my entire body shaking. I held my breath. I pressed.

"Oh *God,*" she screamed as she bucked against my hand.

I found her clit with my other hand, pinched it, rolled it in my fingers, then soothed it with gentle circular strokes.

She sat up, panting, her fingers clamped around my wrist between her legs. "Do it. Do it. God, I need you."

I pulled my thumb in tight to my palm, pushed my hand into her up to the knuckles, and waited for the moment when she started to come. "Look at me."

She lifted nearly blind eyes to mine—open, vulnerable, trusting.

I rubbed her clit harder, faster, then eased off to feather-light strokes—over it, under it, around the sides—and—*there*—as her hips rose, her legs and stomach contracting with the first wave of orgasm, I slid my hand the rest of the way inside her.

I fucked her. Not hard, but a slow, steady back-and-forth motion, driving the orgasm deep into her, through her, out the other side.

"Don't stop. Don't stop." Her hands clutched the sheets, her head swept from side to side, her eyes wide and fixed on my face.

I wouldn't stop now—couldn't stop now. Sweat dripped from my face, my breasts, onto her heaving belly, and still I kept going, gently, relentlessly. "I love you, I love you," I whispered, over and over.

Now, I could take her to the place she needed to be, beyond the boundaries she hadn't intended to build and didn't know how to break. She let me take her there because she's mine and I'm hers. And that's the only thing I'll ever need to know.

THE EDGE OF TRUST

K eep your eyes on me."
The voice held familiar echoes, but the tone held a note of cold command that struck in the pit of her stomach like a closed fist. Or perhaps it was merely the lack of any emotion whatsoever where she'd come to expect warmth and tenderness that brought acid rising from her depths into the back of her throat.

I said I wanted this. So did she. We sought it. We agreed.

"Did you hear what I said?"

Silently, she swallowed and stared straight ahead at her lover, who lounged in a large leather armchair ten feet in front of her. She had to look down slightly, not just because of her height but because she was standing on a raised platform in the center of a dimly lit room. She was also completely naked. A shaft of pale light from a single spot just above her head cast her tautly etched muscles in bas relief, a living statue, still as death.

Her lover, just visible at the juncture of light and shadow, looked totally at ease in a turquoise silk shirt the same lustrous color as her eyes. The fact that it was unbuttoned its entire length and that she was wearing nothing else appeared not to faze her. She reclined slightly in the depths of the soft cushions, her arms outstretched along the curved arms of the chair, her legs parted only enough to reveal a faint hint of dusty gold.

Her lover waited until she met the turquoise gaze, until she was in her power, before she spoke again.

"Restrain her."

Anticipating, but not truly able to *know* what to expect, she tried to keep breathing, struggled to concentrate on the fleeting reassurance in her lover's face that flickered and was rapidly extinguished as another woman she couldn't quite see moved quickly around her in the semidarkness. She jumped when a hand touched her hip, but she followed the unspoken directions and took a step backward. A moment later she found herself spread-eagled, arms and legs stretched wide by soft leather shackles attached to short chains that ran somewhere beyond her vision. A padded pole was at her back. Her lover was all she could see. When she shifted slightly, the chains grew tight, bringing her up short. She was exposed, helpless, her skin glowing with the first flush of arousal tinged with apprehension. Her lover's eyes were hot. She shivered almost imperceptibly when heat, liquid and heavy, trickled along her thighs.

"She has a beautiful body, doesn't she?" her lover remarked almost clinically. "Run your hands over her—see for yourself."

As the stranger smoothed a hand over her torso, tracing the curves of her small breasts before drawing down the center of her belly, she watched her lover flick the shirt off her chest and caress her fingers lovingly over her own breasts. She hadn't known what to expect, but *oh God not this! The icy distance, the searing connection.* When she saw her lover's nipples stiffen, her stomach muscles twitched, first in surprise, then with quick jerks of lust.

Nothing excited her as much as her lover's excitement.

Lips, soft and moist, sucked at the skin just below her navel. Sighing involuntarily at the swift jolt of hot pleasure, she didn't look at the stranger who touched her; only her lover mattered. She knew what that sleek, firm body—that smooth, hot skin—felt like beneath her hands, and her clitoris stiffened at the sight of her lover sensuously circling her nipples before stroking slowly down to the gold at the base of her belly, hips lifting slightly to greet the practiced caress. Despite the bonds that held her, she leaned forward, unconsciously offering herself, all the while imagining *her* hands claiming her lover.

Then her lover smiled, eyes dreamy but voice still commanding. "Now her nipples."

"Oh!" she cried sharply as fingers grasped, then twisted—first one, then the other. Her hips convulsed as the electric sensation shot ruthlessly between her legs. Moisture seeped steadily between her thighs. "Lover?" she questioned uncertainly, voice unsteady, as her body responded to the stranger's manipulations. *I can't help it. It's making me wet.*

They'd sought this. Agreed. But her desire was like an uninvited guest in the night, unbidden and strangely unwelcome. She'd never been so ready to surrender and never before needed permission so much. "Lover?"

"Squeeze harder," her lover instructed huskily, both hands palming her breasts, forcing them together, fingers tugging ruthlessly at the reddened nubs.

Groaning, fire curling in the pit of her stomach, streaking along her spine, she twisted against her restraints. Frantic to escape the tormenting hands, desperate for more. "Oh yes, please...stop... yes...oh..."

"Kneel in front of her," her lover ordered, dropping one hand between her legs and trailing her fingers up and down her inner thighs. The silky skin glistened in the light. "Work on her legs, but don't go near her clit."

Moaning steadily now as hands kneaded the muscles in her buttocks and thighs, she arched her back, no longer trying to contain the pleasure. Her clitoris throbbed painfully, sharply demanding attention. Quivering, mesmerized by the sight of her lover slipping slick folds of swollen flesh lazily between her fingers, she thrust mindlessly against the chains that held her prisoner. When she heard her lover cry out softly, saw trembling fingers brush against the base of the exposed clitoris, she felt her own body clench deep inside. Their passion danced in tandem, pulse for aching pulse. *Stroke yourself, lover. Do it, you know you want to, do it, do it—*

"Touch me," she whispered without meaning to speak.

"Oh no, baby," her lover murmured, hips thrusting gently. "You don't want it bad enough yet."

I do! Oh God, I want to come so bad.

She sobbed, hips jerking in the air, desperate for her lover's touch. When a finger explored lightly between her legs, sending flames bursting from her clitoris into her pelvis, the first tantalizing whisper of approaching orgasm fluttered through her belly. If she pushed forward just a little, that finger would touch her hard enough to make her come. She didn't know she was whimpering as she fought against the leather and steel.

"Please," she begged, her clitoris twitching ceaselessly and the promise of relief so near. She dangled impotently in the restraints, watching through heavy eyelids as her lover spread her legs farther, resting her knees over the wide leather arms to expose her desire. "*Please.*"

"Stroke her clit," her lover demanded hoarsely, doing the same to herself. "Be careful with it. She'll come if you work her too long. And I *don't* want her to come!"

"I need to," she pleaded. "I'm ready now, lover. I need to come."

"Mmm, baby, you beg so sweet. Oh! Mmm, yeah..." Her lover's fingers were a blur. "Not yet. Not yet."

Helplessly, she tried to focus on her lover, but she was losing the struggle for control. She didn't care who was touching her any longer, as long as the touch didn't stop. If she didn't come soon she was going to implode. "No more," she begged. "I can't stand it. Oh, yes...touch me there...harder...please make me come..."

"You are...not to come...without permission," her lover gasped, flicking her clitoris rapidly up and down.

Too late—I'm gonna come. Gotta come. A captive of her own need, she merely grunted, jerking desperately against the fingers that tormented her.

"Faster, squeeze her harder," her lover managed, breathing unevenly through clenched teeth, twisting on the chair, legs outstretched and rigid. "She loves that."

"Lover, oh...she's making me come!" She panted, stomach hard, ready to explode. "Oh, can I—"

"Lick her!"

She wailed as the warm, soft tongue ran the length of her, ending with one long, firm caress from the underside of her clitoris and around the pulsing head. With the last ounce of strength she possessed, she sought her lover's face through eyes nearly blind with need. "Please...oh please...is it all right?"

"Yes, baby—yes—" her lover screamed, tugging her clitoris frantically. "Oh, baby, come with me. Oh! Oh, I'm coming!"

As her mind went white, the stranger reached up, grasped her hips, and sucked her all the way into her mouth. With hands clenched into fists beyond the restraining cuffs, bound by need and imprisoned by desire, she jammed herself against the woman's face. Head thrown back, the tendons in her neck standing out in tight cords, she shouted as the wrenching spasms tore her apart.

For an instant, the only sounds were those of their joint release reverberating throughout the room. Then, there was nothing but the whisper of soft sobbing.

"Get her down," her lover gasped weakly. "Be careful."

When she collapsed to her knees, shattered by more than pleasure, swaying on the edge of trust, her lover was there to shelter her in loving arms.

MEETING FtF

I pace restlessly on the corner opposite the small coffee bar in Old City. The few small, round, glass-topped tables set out in front of the tiny establishment on the uneven red-brick sidewalk leave barely enough room for passersby to get around them without stepping into the cobblestone street. *Street* is a generous term for what is little more than an alley, but the history-laden district with its three-hundred-year-old buildings has its charms. All of which are lost on me as I watch the café for some sign of her. No one is seated at the tables.

I'm fifteen minutes early. Still lots of time to think about the fact that she might not show up at all and to worry that I haven't dressed appropriately for the occasion if she does. Plenty of time to spend trying *not* to think about the possibility that she won't want me—in the flesh. Nine months into our relationship, and *now,* fifteen minutes before liftoff, I get to worry about that.

Funny how it's all turned around. Usually it's the chemistry, that elusive indescribable irrational spark that gets things started. You see someone hot and give her a look. She looks back, and you're on your way. You spend a little time finding out if there's any more to it than heat, or you have a quick, sweaty tumble, but either way—you *know*. Then you go on from there, discovering, exploring, learning. Or you smile, say it was nice, and move on. Not this time. Now I'm in so deep I can't breathe, and I've never seen her face, heard her voice. Well, I know her "voice"—the cadence of her speech, the words she uses when she's angry or happy or horny. I can tell from the length of her sentences if she's stressed or tired or ready for loving.

And she knows me in ways I never thought possible and had given up hoping for.

She knows practically all there is that's worth knowing about me. My passions. My hopes. My dreams. What I fear; what I love. How I like to come. I know almost all those things about her, too— what makes her laugh, what makes her cry, what makes her come. I know she can turn me inside out with a word. Or the absence of one. Silence has become my greatest fear. Even anger is better than that. Because when I don't hear from her, I am afraid that she is gone forever.

Although I can't remember who suggested it first, we both agreed that it was time. Time to make the final connection. Time to meet. Because there was too much between us to contain inside the perimeter of a four-hundred-square-inch, high-resolution monitor any longer. We have five senses, and there is only so long that the critical ones can be denied. I had to hear her voice, touch her skin, smell her scent, and taste her desire. Or die from the deprivation.

And now that I'm about to see her for the first time, at the same instant she sees me, I don't know if I'll pass the test. She has written that she likes androgynous women. Anxiously I wonder just *how* androgynous she really meant. I catch a glimpse of myself as I pass the wide plate-glass window in the storefront café—a pale blue denim (pressed and fitted) work shirt, low-cut button-fly jeans, black Doc Martens twelve-eye boots. No tie. Thought the tie might be a little too much even for a liberated, out lesbian artist like her. My hair is as long as I let it get before it needs to be trimmed— almost to the collar in back, long enough on the sides to brush the brown mixed with gray at the temples back into casual layers. I run a hand through the unruly wave at the front that wants to fall over my forehead. It does. The gold signet ring on my small finger catches the light, glints back at me from the glass, and I survey the rest of the picture. Very thin-rimmed, tortoiseshell glasses—the professor look. Athletic build, not much heavier than when I was eighteen. On a good day I can still wear the same size jeans. Not bad, I guess, but I'm still nervous—she's younger—a lot younger. She might have fallen in love with my quick wit and irresistible charm, but I'm hoping to impress her in the flesh. Soon.

I check the street sign, double-check the address. Right name engraved on the discreet wooden sign hung above the door. This is the right coffee shop, all right. I take one of the sidewalk tables where I can keep watch in both directions without looking as if I'm at a tennis match. I try to amuse myself by observing the interplay of students, faculty, and staff passing by from the nearby campus. Snippets of conversation and laughter float to me on the warm afternoon breeze. I feel a little out of body. *What the hell am I doing meeting a stranger who might just have been playing an elaborate game with me for the last three-quarters of a year?* But she couldn't have been, could she? There are some things you just can't fake. Need is one of them.

Check my watch—five minutes to four. We'd agreed on four o'clock. We'd agreed no pictures. I know she'll be early. I know I'll recognize her. If I leave now, she'll understand. And I'll lose my mind wondering what could have been.

I watch the street. I see her now, crossing the intersection with an expectant expression—excited, it appears to me. She sure doesn't look as nervous as I feel. My height, but definitely not androgynous. Lustrous, windblown hair—thick and dark—almost to her shoulders. From here, I can't see the beginnings of gray I know are there. She told me about that right after I finally confessed my age. Maybe to make me feel better. White T-shirt—very white, no wrinkles, nice tits. Very nice. Jeans—not tight, but fitted enough to show off a tight butt and strong thighs. She's sexy and moves like she knows it; my pulse shoots up a notch. Our eyes meet—she grins. So do I. I stand up as she approaches. I watch her walk—confident, centered—all the time her looking me over, taking her time with it, too. Cocky. I knew that about her—love her for it. But then, love isn't the issue here.

I let her look, want her to look, hoping—Christ, *praying*—the packaging will do. Because this time I want to fuck her, skin on skin. She stops a few feet away, smiles with her eyes. Then her whole face lifts as she smiles with her mouth—a generous, very kissable mouth. I want her so much right then. Her eyes are very bright, shining, brilliant. I'm drowning.

"Hi," she says softly, even a little shyly. *That* surprises me.

"Hi," I answer, my throat tight.

"You look great."

"So do you." *Jesus. So do you.* I clear my throat. Try not to shake. Gesture to the table. "You hungry?"

There's no way I could possibly eat. All I want is to touch her. She shakes her head, her hand trailing lightly down my arm, brushing over my hand, taking my fingers in hers. Her skin is warm, her gaze so steady.

"Yes."

I try not to look disappointed.

She tugs my hand, pulls me around the table into the little street. "Come with me."

I follow. I would have gone anywhere as long as she held my hand. We walk, our shoulders touching, our strides well matched. We don't talk. We don't need to. There is no need to say what we both know in our souls. Love was never the issue here.

She climbs four stone steps worn down in the middle from decades of use and opens the door to a three-story, two-hundred-year-old townhouse sandwiched among a row of them, all converted now to apartments. I'm right behind her, almost brushing against her ass. She turns to me as I move to shut out the world, but before I have the door completely closed, my back is against the wall and she's pressing along the entire length of my body. I kick the door the rest of the way shut as her weight pins me. If she's worried about offending my butch sensibilities with a frontal assault, she sure doesn't show it. She's kissing me, and I'm kissing her back— hard, openmouthed, tongue-probing kisses that say *you belong to me*. We're both gasping, groaning softly at the physical sensations that are so damn familiar and so completely new. I pull her shirt out, slide my hands up. No bra—she did that for me. Another reason I adore her. She remembers what I need. Her nipples are already hard but they stiffen further as I clamp down on them, both at once, my hands cupping her breasts, squeezing. She moans and twitches and pushes into my palms.

"Apartment?" I ask desperately. This can't be smart, fucking in the hallway like this, but my brain is melting fast.

"Yeah," she gasps. Her hand fisted in my shirtfront, she dances and drags me ten steps further along the dim corridor. Then, with my hand still tormenting her nipples, she produces a key from somewhere, turns a lock, and we tumble into a room. Two more steps and I bang up against the back of something—a couch, I think. She's got her hands on my ass, massaging my butt roughly, pulling me closer, fitting thigh between thighs, pelvis to pelvis, our mouths still fused.

Then she gasps, pulls her mouth from mine, and leans back in my arms to stare at me. She blushes. I have my hands on her nipples, she's feeling me up—and *now* she blushes. God, she's beautiful. I nudge the hard curve against her crotch a little, and her eyes widen as she realizes she really *did* feel what she thought she felt.

"Okay?" I whisper, holding my breath, praying again.

She slides a hand around my thigh—between my legs—finds the cock, and cups it in her hand.

"*Okay,*" she murmurs, leaning to kiss me again.

She tugs it, my clit surges to twice its size, and my knees get so weak I almost fall down. She laughs. Quick learner. Still working the cock around in my pants, she gets her other hand on the front of my jeans and starts pulling the buttons open. I've got it easier. Her jeans zip.

I get her fly down in record time and push the denim down over her hips. No underwear either. She's more than a dream; she's a miracle. When her hand dips into my fly, I toss my head back and groan. There isn't much room in there with her fingers and the cock and my clit all smashed together, and I'm feeling every little movement of her fingers straight through to my spine. I look down, wide-eyed, as she fists me inside my jeans.

"Jesus!"

"Mmm, nice." She tilts her head, her eyes dreamy as she searches my face. "I want to jerk you off. Can I?"

I cover her hand from the outside, stopping the torment. "No... I mean, yes...you can, for sure but...I mean...not yet."

"Can I take it out?"

My head is about to come off. "Oh yeah, please."

She eases it free, kissing me again, pinning me to the sofa back this time. The length of it lies along my belly now, between us, as she surges against me again and again. The base pounds my clit as she pumps her hips into me. She's naked to midthigh, her T-shirt tented up over my hands, her bare belly rubbing over mine as she slides all over the dick.

Jesus! Who's fucking whom here? Stupid question. She owns me. Has from the first.

She's groaning as she bites my neck, kisses my jaw, my chest, my nipples through my shirt—I'm damn near coming from the sensations assaulting me everywhere at once. Someone is whimpering—I think it's me. My legs are turning to rubber and there's a dangerous quivering in my belly.

Fuck! She's gonna make me come.

"Baby, wait!" I cry.

She eases her hips away from me.

Oh God—I don't know what I want, but not that!

I start to protest; she laughs again. Then she shoves her hand between us and tugs my dick. "Are you going to fuck me with that thing or just tease me all night?"

My clit twitches like crazy when she says that. God, *I'm* crazy about her. She lets me turn her so it's her butt against the sofa now and I'm between her legs.

"Step out of your jeans," I growl as I drop to my knees, my cock brushing her leg as I move down. My hands part her thighs, my lips find her clit. She cries out in surprise. I groan, my stomach clenching at the first taste of her. She's so wet, so sweet, so goddamned perfect. Her clit is hard, waiting for my tongue, my lips. I suck it in, tug at the inner lips with my teeth, bite gently. She grabs my head, pumps against my face erratically. Her body is calling the shots, and I follow her rhythm. I'm licking the whole length of her, trying to swallow every drop of sweet come, stroking under the stiff shaft, up over the top, around the sides. The muscles of her sex contract.

"I need to come soon." Her voice is high and tight, her fingers twitching in my hair.

She needs to come, all right, and I want her on the edge. I'm about to go over mine. Still licking her, I rub my clit under the cock. It's huge, heavy, throbbing. If I stroke it another few seconds I'm gonna be coming all over her. I'm close to forgetting why I should wait.

"Please, please, please," she sighs, her head rolling gently from side to side. "Fuck me, make me come...fuck me, make me come...fuck me fuck me..."

I'm so close to exploding I'm not sure I can even get it *in* her without coming. Standing on shaking legs, I grit my teeth, grab the cock, and guide the head between her thighs. Rub it against her clit—she whimpers, grabs my ass, tries to pull me into her. I spread my legs, tilt my pelvis forward, and angle the cock up with my hand. She feels it, helps me, her fingers on mine—leading me home. Between us we slide the cock in.

My head is pounding, and she's making little wild noises in the back of her throat. I can't stop my hips from pumping. I'm gasping and groaning and fucking her for all I'm worth. She's got her arms around my neck and she's fucking me right back, the both of us poised to come, neither wanting to give in. Her muscles finally squeeze down on the cock so hard that when I go to pull out for a long stroke, it doesn't come—so I just slam back into her, and my clit goes crazy.

"Ah fuck, I'm gonna come!"

My pelvis hits her clit, the cock bangs deep into her, working that spot that's sending her over. She bites my shoulder, trying not to scream. I'm coming now, can't stop it—great pounding waves shooting from my clit, rising through my belly into my chest. I shout meaningless words, jerking in her arms—inside her, and she screams. Screams and screams and comes all over my cock.

God, she's beautiful when she comes—her whole body resonates with the sound and fury of it. Her climax seems to go on forever, and with each contraction she moans, digging her fingers into my ass.

I'm afraid I'll crush her I'm holding on so tight, still coming in slow rolling spasms. With my mouth close to her ear, I murmur, "I love you."

"I know," she whispers brokenly, still coming. "I love you."

But we both already knew that. Love was never the issue here.

SOUL ON DISPLAY

They say that presentation is as important as the meal.

Actually, there are times when presentation isn't just important, it's everything—when you need to whisper your desire without words; when you need to bare your soul in silence; when you need to be known without explanation.

Tonight is one of those nights. Tonight I need for you to know my need, my desire, my helpless devotion. I've missed you.

I shower carefully, washing my hair, covering every part of my body with creamy, vanilla-scented suds, shaving my legs and underarms smooth. My thighs need no attention, being essentially hairless, but I do consider trimming the soft strands of pale red between them...for a minute or two. I'm pretty fond of it, and you always say you like to work through it, searching out my heat, my wetness, my pulsing clit. I leave it.

Just imagining your fingers parting me, sliding over the edges of my desire, makes my clit throb. I see you grinning as I groan and raise my hips in a desperate plea for you to touch me. "I'm so hard. Please stroke it—make me come." I see you laugh as you deny me, flicking the hood once as you draw away.

"Do it yourself," I hear you whisper as you lean back to watch me quiver and shudder.

I love to come for you. When you touch me; when you tell me to touch myself. But I won't. Not today. Today I need it to be you.

I dry myself, taking care not to linger near sensitive areas. When I'm this ready the merest touch will make me wet, and I'm saving that for later. Yet I know as I pull the soft, well-broken-in leather pants over my naked legs that I will be dripping before I get the zipper closed. The ridged seam presses against my clit. It is already stone hard. It will be harder still before this is over. With every step, the stiff shaft rubs against the second skin encasing my crotch, and my belly aches with the merciless need to get off. I want to squeeze it, just to ease the pressure. I don't. Can't. I want to come so bad, sweet wanting that only you can ease.

Christ, I hope you don't decide to work late. I'll melt down in the living room if I have to wait too much longer.

I wear no shirt, no shoes, no jewelry. I am only a body—bare breasts, bared soul, powerless need encased in black leather.

I hear the key turn. The room is nearly in shadow; the only light comes from the subdued lamps in the adjoining bedroom. It is enough for you to see me, and for me to see your face. There is nothing else tonight—my body, your eyes.

"Don't turn on the lights," I say as your arm precedes you into the foyer, searching the wall for the switch. Your hand stills in midair. I hear a swift intake of breath. You are thinking rapidly, calculating your next move from the tone of my voice. You're so good at that. You always know.

I stand, my butt resting against the rounded back of the sofa, waiting. Part of me is praying. Can you feel my need in the dark, hear my desire in the stillness? Or is this the time you won't know? Is this the time I'll be left to drown beneath the weight of my silence?

The door closes, your briefcase goes quietly to the floor, and you move closer with deliberate steps. You study me, not brazenly, not boldly, but through still, calm, steady eyes. I gaze back, trying to give nothing away. My trembling hands rest on the leather sofa back as I present myself, exposing so much more than flesh. The air between us crackles with the sound of our unspoken words.

You look into my eyes, flicker a smile, and part your lips with a soft sigh. I tilt my hips ever so slightly in invitation. *Can you hear me, baby? I've been so lonely.*

Your eyes return to mine, and the certainty in yours before you lower your gaze—down the plane of my chest, over my belly, to my crotch—eases the tightness around my heart. When you kneel between my parted legs and press your hands in the center of each black-clad thigh, I draw my first free breath in what feels like days. The muscles in my belly clench at the first faint touch. When you press your face to the leather covering my crotch, hard enough for me to feel it in my clit, a warning tingle ripples down my legs. I swallow a moan, try not to pump against you. I want it to last; I want to come so bad; I want to hide my secrets a few moments longer. I look down, watch you through the haze of want clouding my mind.

Your hands come to my fly; you slide the zipper down, spread the material, grip the waistband and pull hard, almost but not quite exposing my clit. The leather rides against the shaft and the sudden pressure almost makes me come. My arms shake with the effort of keeping myself upright. I am holding my breath, struggling not to move. Your arms circle to the rear, knead my ass, pull me hard against your face. When your chin strikes my stiff clit, trapped by soft leather, I close my eyes against the torment. I am dying; I am silent. I need you to know what I need.

With the stiff tip of your tongue, you flick the hood where it joins my body. My clit jumps under your tongue, twitches unbearably beneath the leather, and I think I might fall. I grip the edges of the sofa harder, straight-arming it, determined to take it for as long as I can. My head is already swimming, my stomach in knots. You press your tongue lower as you slowly draw the leather down, running along each side of the shaft, then rocking it back and forth. I bite my lip. I taste blood. I am poised to come, have been for hours, but I knew you would make me wait. Need you to make me wait. I want you to make me come.

You tug my pants to the floor, press your shoulders between my legs, parting them, opening me. Your tongue slides down into the folds between my legs, releasing a flood of passion down your face. While I watch through a cloudy haze, you lick it greedily, making a sound deep in your throat that almost makes me come. When you bring your thumb up to spread my lips, dive deep into me with your mouth, I fear I'll lose it. It hurts to breathe; my thigh muscles are shaking, cramping. I am choking on a groan that threatens to become a wail. I need your mouth so much. I need you to take me inside you.

You suck the tender lips into your mouth, pulling gently, moving your head from side to side, playing with them. Your thumb caresses the muscled opening between my buttocks, round and round, coaxing me to relinquish the last barrier. I whimper—I can't help it.

You must hear it, but you have the decency not to laugh. You allow me to believe that I am still in control. You are so good at this—you pretend I am in charge, but we both know that the power has nothing to do with our position. You command me from your knees. And when you claim me with your thumb, I buck against your mouth, almost coming. I am so sensitive there—the pressure surges into my clit like a hammer blow. I didn't think I could get any harder, but I do. It hurts I'm so stiff now. My hips jerk, I gasp, but I keep my eyes open, focus on your eyes watching me, and will myself to hold on. The entire surface of my body is tingling. I'm suspended by a thread from the edge of orgasm, my clit painfully swollen, my internal muscles contracting spasmodically, my ass clenched around your thumb. Do it now—don't make me tell you. I want you to take what is yours.

Finally, oh God *finally*, you take pity on me. As you're fucking my ass, your tongue rapidly licks my clit—under the hood, up and down the shaft, across the exposed tip. My head snaps back, a strangled cry escapes me, and I can't hold on to my silence. I start to come—wave upon wave of gripping, pulsing, mind-wrenching explosions shooting from the base of my clit, screaming outward, consuming me. Defenseless, I'm falling. You hold me up, strong arms wrapped tightly around my thighs.

"Baby, don't stop," I plead, still coming so hard.

The first words spoken.

You lift your lips from me for an instant.

"Never," you whisper before you suck me into your mouth again.

You always know.

HAPPY, HAPPY BIRTHDAY, BABY

I first got the idea while she was lying on top of me, naked, and I was about to come. I don't usually do a lot of thinking in that position at that *particular* moment, but there was something about the way she sounded that pulled me out of the fog of my own pleasure to focus on her. As I often do when my mind is dissolving and my muscles are about to shred from my bones, I dug my fingers into her wonderfully round, astonishingly tight ass, clamped my legs around her rugby-player thighs, and screamed in her ear, "Please, baby, please! Make me come!"

She pumped her hips harder, banging her pelvis into my clitoris just the way I liked it when I was about to shoot into the heavens, and then, with her sweat-streaked face pressed to my neck, she moaned, "Oh God, how I wish I could fuck you."

There was something almost forlorn in the choked, nearly desperate timbre of her voice that stayed with me all through the heaving spasms in my belly and the blessed uncoiling of the tension that had tied my nerve endings into jangling knots. Nothing could stop me from coming, or diminish the toe-curling pleasure, but as I quieted, I still heard the echo of sadness in her words. It wasn't the first time she'd said that she wanted to fuck me, or intended to fuck me, or was about to fuck me, but it was the first time she'd ever said it that I knew she meant it literally. I stroked her neck and back and whispered, "What do you need, baby? Huh? What do you need?"

She shivered against me, trembling like a fine thoroughbred after the race was run, and laughed softly. "Only you." She lifted her head, her face all flushed and triumphant, with that look she gets when she's pleased with herself. While she grinned at me, her dark eyes all smoky and soft, she shifted one leg over my thigh and rocked against me until she came, her eyes still open and fixed on mine. Then it was as if the strength went out of her and she collapsed and let me hold her. She doesn't do that all that often. Sometimes when she's very tired or like now, when she's all mine.

You'd think after almost a year, I'd know if there was something she needed in bed. As I lay there with her weight upon me, her heart thundering against my breasts, I realized that I'd never thought to ask. We'd always seemed to fit together so well, from the very first time. That in and of itself was unusual, because I'd found over the years that it often took more than a few tries for someone to figure out how to trip my triggers. Not so with her. She had the hands of a magician, the mouth of a saint, and she could read me as if I were a billboard lighting up the night in Times Square. Even though I'll admit that I'm usually in a pre- or post-orgasmic haze most of the time that we're in bed together, I certainly would've noticed before now if she weren't getting off. True, she had a habit of taking charge, and I can't say I minded since she was so damn good at it, but there wasn't an inch of her fine form that I hadn't had my hands or my mouth on at one point or another. Until that night, I'd never thought there was anything else she might need.

"Baby?"

"Hmm," she muttered, all drowsy and adorable.

"If there was something I wanted you to do in bed, would you do it?"

"Sure." She stirred faintly and raised her head. "Is there?"

I grabbed the hair at the back of her neck and tugged her head back down on my shoulder. "If I think of something, I'll let you know."

"Okay."

"If there was something *you* wanted, you'd tell me, right?"

"Uh-huh." She burrowed her face against my breast and idly sucked on my nipple. The last thing I thought before I slipped back into that "going to have to come again" mist was that maybe she didn't *know* there was something she wanted.

"Can I ask a dumb question?" my best friend Cindy asked me as we pushed through the noontime lunch crowds on Walnut Street and headed west toward the Pleasure Chest.

"What?"

"Shouldn't this be something you're doing with your girlfriend?" Cindy swerved to avoid a throng of tourists in the middle of the sidewalk, cameras pointed toward Rittenhouse Square. "I mean, after all, it is something...you know...for the *two* of you."

"It's a surprise." I just hoped it was going to be a good one.

"Well, okay. I can see that. But you know, this isn't exactly my area of expertise."

I gave her a look. "As a dyed-in-the-wool straight girl, I should think you'd know a *lot* about it."

She smirked, her cute pixie face taking on a very satisfied expression. "Well, I don't make a study of it as long as it's getting the job done."

I started down the narrow basement stairs to the black-painted door of the Pleasure Chest and said over my shoulder, "Well, that's exactly what I need you for. To make sure it's gonna get the job done."

Since the place was only open noon to eight, and my girlfriend's birthday was the next day, I prayed they'd have everything I needed. Mail-order was not an option. We were the only customers in the shop, and to my great relief, the salesperson was a woman. Actually, a cute young chick with an eyebrow piercing, wearing a great deal of leather that didn't cover much of anything, and a friendly smile.

"Hiya. Looking for anything special?"

I pointed. Cindy got to within six inches of the shelf and said, "*Cool.*"

The salesgirl came around from behind the counter and joined us in front of the row of multicolored, multishaped, and multisized cocks. Addressing us both, she said, "Which one of you is going to be wearing it most of the time?"

Apparently, cocks are no longer reserved for the butches among us. Cindy's face split into an enormous grin. I said, "It's for my girlfriend. No, not her. My *girlfriend* girlfriend."

"Oh, I get it. You're just girlfriends."

"Right," Cindy and I said simultaneously.

"So are we talking a harness here, a packing dick, or just a handheld?"

I must have looked blank because Cindy piped up. "They want to fuck."

"Okey-dokey. Then we're going to need a harness." She looked at me. "How's your girl built?"

"A few inches taller than me, a few pounds lighter."

"A regular harness will work, then. Personally, I prefer buckles over snaps, because they're more adjustable." She pulled something down from the wall and held it up. "What do you think about this? It's the most popular."

Considering that there were several straps extending from a triangular piece of leather with a hole in the middle about the size of...well, a cock...it wasn't too hard to figure out how the thing worked. Cindy was all over it in a flash.

"Oh, this is sexy," she said breathily, holding it up in front of her crotch.

Just the idea of it *under* that expensive silk surface gave me a little zing, and the image of a cock tenting the smooth line of her skirt had my head hurting. In a good way. I blinked and grabbed the contraption away from her. I did *not* need to think about my best friend with a strap-on under her skirt. I held it up and judged the width, mentally picturing my girlfriend's hips. That picture did nothing for the blood that insisted on pooling between my legs.

"This looks good." Deliberately, I ran my gaze along the assortment of upright cocks. No way was I buying a Day-Glo pink dildo or one that resembled anything that swam in the ocean. I pointed to an anatomically correct model in a nice subtle shade of green. Understated but elegant. "That one seems nice."

"It is." The salesgirl picked it up and wrapped her fingers around it, jiggling it as she talked. "It's relatively comfortable to wear..." She demonstrated by bending it in the middle. "But stiff enough for penetration." She didn't demonstrate that part. "But it's sorta on the short side and if your girlfriend's fairly...vigorous, it's likely to fall out at just the wrong time." She raised a questioning eyebrow at me. Cindy regarded me with rapt attention.

"Uh, in that case, something longer might be better."

"Now *this* one," she indicated as she returned the green and picked up another in dark blue with a lovely swirl of white, "is good because it has these ridges right near the base that rub against your clit. If you tend to come mostly from clitoral stimulation, it's great."

If Cindy's eyes got any brighter, flames were going to shoot out.

"I'll take it," I said hastily.

"Wait a minute," Cindy interjected. "It's not just length that makes a difference." She held out her hand and the salesgirl dutifully plunked the dildo into it. "Width is important, too." Cindy closed her fingers around it as she shut her eyes.

For one terrifying second, I thought she was going to start giving it a hand job. Instead, she just made a little humming noise and nodded.

"This seems about right." She gave me another little smirk. "If you get really lucky." Then she tilted her head and gave the line of dildos an appraising glance. "So...ever get straight couples shopping for these?"

"All the time," the salesgirl said knowingly.

I left with the very tasteful blue cock. Cindy, of course, went for the neon pink. Some unsuspecting guy was going to get very lucky this weekend.

It was almost two in the morning before I was able to get the last partygoers out of my apartment. All night long, Cindy gave me the high sign and a grin that told me she had definitely swallowed the canary. Or someone had. I tried really hard not to look at the guy she was with while thinking about what they might have done in bed that afternoon.

Once we were alone, my girlfriend flopped onto the bed, fully clothed, with a groan. "God, I'm beat."

I sat beside her and ran my hand up and down the inside of her leg, hooking my nails over the seam that curved along her crotch. Her hips gave a little lift and she made an appreciative sound low in her throat when I lingered there a little longer than anywhere else. "Did you have a nice birthday, baby?"

She smoothed her hand up my nearly bare back to the thin silk tie that held the halter top in place. Deftly, she loosed the knot, caught the bit of material with her clever fingers, and eased the garment away to leave me bare from the waist up. Then she rolled onto her side and tugged me down to face her. Nuzzling my neck as she palmed my breast, she murmured, "The best. You looked so sexy all night, I couldn't wait for everyone to go."

My breath was getting short and my mind a little fuzzy as she toyed with my nipple, alternately tugging and squeezing it. This wouldn't do. I shifted away as subtly as I could and decided distraction was the best weapon. I cupped her crotch and did a little squeezing of my own. She might be butch, but she's far from stone. She moaned and covered my fingers with hers, pressing down on my hand while she lifted her hips.

"Baby?" I asked quietly.

"Mmm?"

"Did you like your presents?" I started a little circular motion as I leaned closer and ran my tongue over her lower lip.

"Uh-huh." She sounded a little dazed.

"When I was a kid, and my brother had a birthday," I tugged at her lip with my teeth, "my mother always got *me* a present so I wouldn't feel left out."

"Oh man," she muttered. She opened her eyes with an expression halfway between worry and want. "Oh hell, honey, I didn't get you anything."

I smiled. She was so cute when she thought she might be in trouble. I tapped a finger on her chin. "That's okay. I got one for myself." Her brows furrowed as I leaned across her and pulled open the bottom drawer of the night table. I took out the carefully wrapped package with the bright blue bow and handed it to her. "Here. This is from you to me."

"I don't get it."

"Open it while I get ready for bed. I'll be back in a minute. You get ready, too."

She looked even more confused as I stood up and walked into the bathroom, closing the door behind me. I gave her five minutes while I got undressed at a leisurely pace. When I opened the door, the first thing I noticed was the candles. The second was her sitting propped up in bed, a sheet drawn up to her waist and her chest bare. The look on her face, all hungry and needy, made me instantly wet. I looked at her lap. I couldn't help it. She had her hands loosely folded over her crotch, and I couldn't see anything. Just thinking about what was under there made my clitoris twitch. The box and rumpled birthday paper sat on the floor, empty, by the side of the bed. She held out her hand.

"Come on over here."

I didn't run to her, but I felt like it. Instead, I walked slowly and sat on the side of the bed, making no move to get under the sheets. Leaning into her, breasts to breasts, I threaded my arms around her neck and kissed her. Oh, she was hungry all right. Her tongue dove into my mouth instantly; her hands were all over me, demanding and possessive. Her desire never failed to ignite mine, and that night she was on fire. She was quivering, like she did when she wanted me and wouldn't stop until she'd demolished me, and I knew what it was from. Without moving my mouth away from hers, I slid my hand under the sheets and down her belly. She jerked and groaned. It was the most natural thing in the world to close my fingers around her cock as she slipped her fingers between my legs. She brushed my wetness over my clitoris and I pushed down on the firmness in my hand, and we both moaned.

"You like my present, baby?" I gasped.

"Oh, Christ, yes."

She pressed her face between my breasts and stroked me faster. I was afraid she'd make me come, and I grabbed her wrist to stop her. "Wait, wait, baby. I want to come with you inside me."

She made a noise that sounded almost like a sob, and I moved my hand from her arm to her hair and pulled her head back so I could see her eyes. "What?"

"I want that so much."

She grinned, shakily, and her eyes shimmered with what I feared were tears. Still gripping her cock with my other hand, I kissed her forehead, her eyes, her mouth. "I love you. You're perfect."

Then I pushed her back against the pillows and threw the sheet aside, looking down as I exposed her. She has a beautiful body, and the cock thrusting up from between her legs neither added nor detracted from that. It *did*, however, look sexy. "Hold it for me," I whispered.

When she reached down and closed her hand around the base, her stomach tightened and her hips twitched, and a shiver ran through me. I loved knowing that having it made her hot; that under that flat, smooth base her clit was rigid and wet. I swung my leg over her body until I straddled her and grabbed the cock with my hand just above hers so that only the head was exposed. With my eyes holding hers, I lowered myself onto her, catching my lip at the first surge of pressure. That fat head hit somewhere just inside me that felt oh so good, and I ached the way I do when I need to come. "Oh God."

"Are you okay?" she asked, her voice low and tight.

I nodded, unable to speak as I took her deeper into me. Until she was buried in me. She kept her hand curled against the base of her cock, and the back of her thumb rubbed against my clitoris. I leaned forward, bracing myself on her shoulders, and started to rock. I couldn't wait; I had to come.

"Can I move?" She sounded a little desperate as she lay rigid beneath me.

"I thought..." I caught my breath as I tightened inside. I was close to exploding already. "I thought you wanted to fuck me."

All I remember is her hands on my hips, guiding me, and my fingers digging into her shoulders as I pistoned and she pumped and I came all over her. When I fell into her arms, she was still inside me. I vaguely registered her reaching down, felt her arm jerking, and knew she was touching herself under the leather. She came fast and hard, whispering my name.

"Oh, sweetheart," she moaned after another minute. "Thank you."

"Happy birthday, baby," I sighed. "Happy, happy birthday."

PLEASURE POINTS

You have a great clit."

"Huh?"

"Seriously." I tilted my head as it rested against your thigh so I could see all the sweeping undulations of tender skin that cradled the upthrust prominence like protective hands. Even unerect, the pale pink, butter-soft tip peeked out beneath the thicker, dark rose hood. "It's beautiful—especially when you're turned on. I love the way it gets so shiny, the head poking out at me when it's hard." I ran my fingertip along the side, pressed deep enough to feel the core, grinning to myself when you gasped.

"Jesus," you whispered when I thumbed the tip gently and your clit twitched.

Mmm, here it comes. Oh yeah, get hard for me, baby.

"And," I continued matter-of-factly, enjoying the power, "I like feeling it swell right before you come." I moved to that spot just underneath that always makes you wet and rubbed—slow and steady. Small circles, not too hard yet. "You get so big then, so stiff righ—"

"You're gonna make me come...if you...keep doing that." Breathless, legs twitching, one hand twisted in the sheets.

"Sorry. I'm just playing around." I eased up on the pressure, slowed my strokes even more. Flick. Flick.

"Oh come on." That tilt of hips I loved, the silent plea for just a little more, just a little harder.

"I'll be good." I really wanted to reach down and stroke my own pulsating clit, but it would be too distracting, and I needed all my concentration to tease you to orgasm. I knew all the signals—I should, we've been lovers for years—but I still needed to listen to the currents of your blood, sense the call of your flesh. Despite how well I knew your body, it still fascinated me. There was both comfort and exhilaration in knowing just how to create desire— how to control the pace, direct the passion, determine the depth and moment of your release. There were times your body demanded to be satisfied immediately—screamed to come—and then I gave you what you needed, just exactly the way you needed it. But there were other times, like now, when I led and you followed, willingly—or not. Dancing to my tune, coming to my song.

"I think you're bigger than me," I mused, switching to long strokes of the shaft between my thumb and finger, squeezing lightly when I got to the tiny ridge just in front of the head. You whimpered. I smiled. My clit beat a frantic rhythm between my thighs, and I clenched my muscles deep inside, holding back the thunder of blood that would soon drive me insane. I started to jerk you off a little faster. "But that's okay—it's a win-win for me. I get your big clit to play wi—"

"You've gotta make me come," you pleaded. "Please, I really need to."

I knew you did. Your clit was stone between my fingers, your legs and ass clenched tight. My fingers were drenched in come, and the beat of your heart pulsed through your clit like hammer blows. I wanted you to come as badly as you did. I couldn't breathe for the beauty of it.

"Ohpleaseplease...right...there...ohyeahbabythat's...just... right...

ohright...there I'm gonnacome...oh yeah oh *yeah*..."

Your clit is gorgeous when it shoots off—dark red, full and hard, jumping against my fingers. If I could, I'd make it do it all day. But now the pressure in my belly was so huge I thought I might scream, and as much as I wanted to keep going, I needed you. I slid up beside you and even though you were still coming, you reached for me.

"You've got a great clit, too," you whispered, your voice raspy, your sweat-dampened face against my neck, your clever fingers already working me to the boiling point.

"Mmm, you make me so crazy," I moaned. Eyes closed, I rubbed my hand over your stomach, found the barbell in your belly button, and tugged on it in time to your fingers jerking my clit. I pulled harder; so did you. "Gonna come."

"Uh-huh."

I twitched at the jewelry, you stroked my clit; I twisted it, you pressed; I rolled it, you squeezed. My fingers flew, so did yours. And then my clit exploded, and I came and came.

"Oh God," I sighed at last, still feebly flicking the piercing in your navel. "You are so good at that."

"You know," you muttered, sleepy and satisfied, softly rubbing my clit. "You work my piercing the way you want me to get you off."

"Yeah?"

"Mm-hmm. Makes me hard when you do that."

I laughed. "Honey, everything does."

"I wonder what would happen if it wasn't in my navel."

I was suddenly wide awake. "Huh?"

"What if it was in my clit?"

"You sure about this?" I asked three nights later as we made our way through the crowds on South Street. There were head shops, piercing parlors, and tattoo places on every block.

"Yeah," you said, blushing cutely. "I've been sorta thinking about it for a long time."

"Well, I know we fooled around talking about it. But this is... a big deal."

"I thought you said it would be sexy." You stopped at the corner of Third and looked into my face. "Don't you want me to?"

"It's not that." I looked away, then sighed and met your worried gaze. "I *really* want you to. But not for me, okay?"

You grinned, your blue eyes clearing. "Okay. I won't let you play with it, then."

I grabbed your hand and pulled you close to the side of a steak joint, angling my body to shield you from passersby, and then gripped your crotch. I squeezed. "Sure about that?"

"Come on," you protested a little desperately. "I have to get naked in a few minutes. Don't make me wet now."

There was something about knowing that my touch made you weak that drove me a little nuts, but I eased up. I knew you were nervous. Hell, *I* was almost nauseous worrying this was going to hurt you. "Okay. But if you want to quit—any time—you just say, and we're done. We'll walk out, no problem, okay?"

"I really want to," you said firmly.

I grinned. "Me, too."

I followed you down the street toward Body Alchemy. It looked typically grungy from the outside—flat-black-painted door, windows frosted so we couldn't see in from the street. When you made up your mind, though, you didn't hesitate. You shouldered through, and I was right on your heels. One long, narrow room, a glass-enclosed counter along one side, a curtained doorway at the end. Behind the counter a youngish guy in a black T-shirt and jeans, piercings in every visible orifice and then some. Both earlobes sported fat glass plugs a half inch in diameter. His nose was pierced, his forehead, his lower lip. I didn't want to, but I imagined what his dick looked like. *Don't go there. Jesus.*

He studied us back, neutrally. I wondered what he thought of two butch dykes in jeans, T-shirts, and boots. He looked from me to you, then settled on you.

"How you doin'?"

"Great," you said, leaning down to look at the jewelry under the surprisingly spotless glass.

"Need something pierced?"

"Uh-huh," you replied absently, staring at the fat silver rings. Fourteen-gauge looked huge to me right about now. You looked up. "My clitoris."

His expression never changed.

"You'll want Venus then—she's the best at that kind of thing."

"Venus," I repeated quietly.

"Yep." He turned to me. "Very experienced. She did my co—"

"Thanks!" I interrupted brightly. I saw you smirk and wanted to slug you. "Is she free?"

At that moment a Tristan Taormino look-alike came through the door in a crotch-high leather skirt, high-heeled boots laced to the knee, and a red tube top that *almost* covered her nipples. Red lipstick, short red-lacquered nails, and big dark eyes. My taste runs to boy-bodies and short-cropped hair, but she made my heart beat a little faster.

"Oh, hey, Venus," the studded guy behind the counter called. "Got a customer here for you."

She looked our way and smiled. "Hi."

Fabulous voice.

"Both of you?"

"Just me," you said.

"Great." She pointed to the curtain at the end of the room. "You ready now?"

I piped up. "I'm coming, too. I'm her lover." Okay, maybe I was just a little more forceful than necessary, but no *way* was she getting her hands on your clit without me in the room.

"Oh, cool," she replied brightly. "Come on back."

The hallway beyond the curtain was narrow and lined with eight-by-ten framed photos of tattooed and pierced body parts. Not people—parts. One penis had half a dozen rings through the undersurface of the shaft and a barbell through the head. Ouch.

"Here we go."

The room was maybe ten by twelve, with a tiny sink in one corner, a padded table in the middle, and a moveable floor lamp in one corner. A box of latex gloves sat beside a series of squat, square stainless-steel trays on the counter by the sink. The room smelled of disinfectant and spices.

"So," she said briskly, indicating the table. "Sit up here a minute and let's figure out what's going to work for you. What kind of piercing do you want?"

"Genital," you said immediately.

"Labia or clitoral?"

"My clit."

I leaned against the counter and stuck my hands in my pockets. It's weird, but they were shaking.

Venus nodded thoughtfully. "You're over eighteen, right?"

We both laughed.

"Had to ask that. And I won't pierce you if you're high."

"Nope. I'm clean and sober."

"Cool." She shifted a little in the smallish space so she could address us both. "What kind of clitoral piercing are you interested in? For show or for sensation?"

"Sensation," we both said together.

"Then you want either a vertical hood, where the jewelry goes under the hood so the ball on the end will rest on the head," she gave us a look to see if we understood, and we both nodded, "or you want a triangle piercing...under the clitoral shaft. The triangle will heighten sexual arousal the most."

"That one," you said without a second's hesitation.

We'd looked at pics on the Internet, read the pros and cons, but I didn't know you'd absolutely decided.

"That's the most serious one we do," Venus advised. "It will hurt a little more and take longer to heal."

"I understand," you said.

"It might make your clit get bigger from the constant stimulation and the healing process—sometimes a *lot* bigger."

You grinned and damn if *my* clit didn't get hard.

"No problem."

Venus nodded. "There are two places I can put it—the standard triangle piercing goes low, where the labia join the hood. Or I can do a deep hood, up high under the base of the shaft. The ring will circle the shaft then."

"Like a little cock ring?" Your voice rose with interest. My clit twitched.

"Uh-huh. If you're built for it." She reached down, opened a drawer in the table, and pulled out a clean white sheet. "Take everything off from the waist down and let's see. You can cover up with the sheet."

While you stripped, she turned on the little spotlight, washed her hands, and pulled on gloves. Then she motioned me over to the table opposite her and gently reached between your legs, parted your labia with the fingers of one hand, and felt your clit. I saw your legs tense, and when she touched your clit, I got a jolt. I love your clit. Even seeing a stranger touch it turns me on. I kept my face completely still.

"Nice," she commented in a surprisingly clinical tone. "You've got a prominent shaft and the hood," she did something with her thumb, and I heard your breath catch, "slides back easily." She straightened. "I can do the deep hood if you want. But that ring is going to keep you erect all the time."

She is anyhow, I thought.

You looked at me, and I rested my fingers on your arm. I knew what you wanted; I always do when it comes to this. "Go for it. If you don't like it, we'll take it out."

"Okay," you said to Venus. "Let's go the whole way."

"I'll put in a fourteen-gauge to start. If you want bigger later, we can change it." She met my gaze. "I have to be sure not to hit the shaft where the nerves run. I need her to be erect so I can tell what's what—it's safer that way. I can do it, or one of you can."

"I'll do it." I didn't even raise my voice this time. I wasn't going to let her or anybody else work you up. Besides, I wanted to be a part of it. I was dying to touch you. "Okay, baby?"

"Yes," you said, your voice husky and low.

Venus turned away and did something in the background with things that clattered quietly. I leaned over, looked into your eyes, and slipped two fingers on either side of your clit. It was instantly hard. I watched your pupils flicker and dance as I carefully rolled the firm core of you between my fingers, pulling slightly at the end of each stroke. I got wet when I felt your warm come glaze my fingertips.

"Don't make me come," you whispered breathlessly.

"I won't," I murmured, but I wanted you just as stiff and swollen as I could get you. I wanted *Venus* to feel exactly where your clit was.

"I'm getting close." There was a note of desperation in your voice and perversely, I wanted to push you closer. You were mine, after all, and in a second I was going to have to hand you over to a strange woman. Your hips lifted and I felt your clit pulse, then go rigid.

"That's it," I said hoarsely, looking up to see Venus across from me. There was a small tray beside her with *things* on it. I didn't look too closely.

"Good." She smiled at you, then me. "Some people orgasm while I'm doing this. It's from the stimulation of the nerves. Don't be embarrassed or anything, okay?"

As she talked, she swabbed something on your thighs, then reached down with one hand. She grasped your clit, then squeezed at the base. The head popped out, and you made a small choked sound.

"You'll probably feel like you need to come as soon as I pierce you. It actually helps ease the discomfort if the clitoris can decompress, so don't fight it."

She reached for something else on the tray, and I looked into your face. A second later, your eyes got wide and you muttered, "Oh, fuck, baby. Oh, I think—Oh!"

You pressed your face to my side. Venus took my hand and placed it gently on your clit.

"Touch her right there. Easy."

I stroked you the way I always did when you were just about to come and you did, sweetly, in slow steady waves, crying out softly with each pulsation. I watched your clit coming. God, it was beautiful. I was always ready to stroke you off, but now...how was I going to keep my hands off you?

When you got your breath back, you pushed up on your elbows and checked yourself out. Grinning, you looked at me. "What do you think?"

"You've got a great clit, baby." I stroked your leg but stayed clear of your piercing. "I don't know how I'm going to stand not being able to play with it for a while, though."

You eyed my crotch. "Good thing we've got a spare."

BOOMERANGING

You're probably familiar with the concept of "round-robin." In the writing trade, it's the sequential addition of chapters or sections to an ongoing—or, more accurately, *evolving*—work by a group of authors. In this particular instance, there were only two of us, and the final product wasn't intended to be a novel, but an anthology. An erotica anthology. And I wasn't certain exactly *who* my writing partner was. Well, I had some idea, since we were both members of the same online writers' group. Nevertheless, we were both cloaked in several layers of online and real-life *noms de guerre*. It was safer, and definitely more titillating, that way. If pressed, I couldn't say exactly when it started. It had sounded simple enough—one of those innocent interactions that occur so naturally in the fluid atmosphere of cyberspace. I said, or maybe she said, "Send me one of yours, and I'll send you one of mine. Maybe someday we can put them together and do a collection. Who knows."

Who knew, indeed.

Seemed like a great idea to me—an exchange of ideas, a stimulus to inspiration, and a chance to share a passion that was hard to explain to someone who didn't do it too. It would be fun. Well, I got that part right; I just hadn't anticipated all the fringe benefits. The first few sections we traded were pretty much as you might expect. A lot of careful comments, a little bit of craft, and now and then, a snippet of playful innuendo. By the third exchange, however, innuendo had segued to suggestion, and flirtation had transformed into seduction. It was one of those things that fed on itself, where the absence of response would have been akin to a cold shower, but a teasing reply resulted in the geometric escalation of sheer unmitigated arousal. Before I knew it, and well before I had the time to understand it, I was in the midst of a full-blown obsession. I can't say I minded. In fact, I'd never enjoyed having my work critiqued so much. I wasn't entirely certain if I was alone in my fixation, and I thought it prudent not to ask. There were boundaries, after all.

I simply decided to allow the words to speak for themselves.

I'd sent my vignette out that morning, so it was my turn to be on the receiving end of the next installment. And knowing that, I'd been stoked for it all day. Talk about Pavlovian response. I heard the little ping and the announcement "You've got mail" and my clit jumped.

The ride home from work in rush-hour traffic was a maddening combination of pleasure and torture, and it had nothing to do with the snarled, slow-moving mass of vehicles. I'd been nearly sick with arousal all day, the kind of stomach-churning, gnawing need that sits heavily between the thighs, begging for relief. My clitoris was a hard, throbbing presence that undercut every thought, dragging my concentration away from what I was supposed to be doing. Even when I was nearly completely absorbed, there—in the background—the drumbeat of desire echoed insistently. The customary half-hour drive crawled past the hour mark, and every few minutes I had to fight the urge to squeeze myself through my jeans. Even self-denial had become satisfying, however, because just as much as I wanted to come instantly—right then and there—I wanted to wait. Prolonging the pleasurable frustration had become a perverse goal in itself. Besides, I couldn't come without the latest episode, not without sacrificing half of the thrill.

Orgasm itself was no longer the goal—well, to be honest, not the *only* goal—because now there was the added enticement of discovering just what line, what phrase, what combination of words might, despite their familiarity, be presented cleverly enough to set me off. Let's just say this had evolved into a form of field study, a serious observation of the effective use of the tools of one's trade. After all, what better way to achieve both enlightenment *and* satisfaction than to become the target of one's own most powerful weapon?

What wonderful webs our words weave.

When I walked into the house, it was all I could do not to sit down in front of the computer immediately. I knew that the message was there waiting, sent from beyond the void, designed to tempt and enthrall me. When I finally allowed myself to look at the monitor, the small rectangular e-mail icon on the toolbar drew my gaze like a magnet. One click—an entire universe just waiting for me to step onto the horizon. I was already breathing heavily, the muscles in my stomach and legs tight with anticipation, when the simmering desire that had been in the background all day suddenly surged and consumed my entire consciousness. I was programmed, every bit as hard wired as the equipment that brought desire and satisfaction to me in the form of silent conversation and intangible caresses. I steadfastly put both hands on the keyboard, out of harm's way, because I so desperately wanted to come.

Scrolling the new messages quickly, I lasered in on the one from anon1102 and groaned in anticipation. Sent at 2:12 p.m. God, salvation had been waiting for over three hours. I was afraid I wouldn't last three minutes. Even as I clicked to open the attachment, I worked open my jeans with the other hand, slid down the zipper, and eased my fingers under the waistband. Not too far just yet, fingertips merely brushing the silk bikinis nestled between my legs. I was wet already, had been all day. I knew without even touching it that my clitoris was swollen to twice its usual size, the tip exposed, so sensitive that just the pressure of my hand above it sent streaks of pleasure curling up into my belly. I needed to be careful. I was too ready already, and it was hard not to press deeper, not to flick the rigid shaft back and forth, not to force the blood to pound even faster through the straining flesh.

I would read, teasing myself, but I would not come.

```
        I'm back from my skate. My skin
is damp, my legs shaking faintly. I
stumble into the shower to rinse away
the residue of dust and sweat. Still
trembling slightly, barely dry, I
stretch out naked on the bed, a towel
under my back, beads of water still
dotting my body. I toss one arm over
my eyes and let my muscles melt into
the firmness beneath me. You come to me
```

```
then, standing for a moment, looking
down, before you press a finger to the
inside of my knee, bidding entrance. I
spread my legs slowly, shifting my hips
to open myself to your view. I haven't
looked at you; you haven't spoken. You
stretch out between my legs, resting
on your elbows, your face inches from
me.
```

It was just the kind of scene I liked. As I read, I couldn't help but imagine being first one, then the other participant, at once touching and watching. It was too much, too much to see, feel, imagine, without joining in. Forcing myself not to jump ahead, I lifted my hips and with one hand pushed down my clothes, trailing my fingers up the inside of my thigh on the way back. The words, a siren's call, guided my touch. I dragged my finger up and down the side of my clitoris, careful to stay away from the fat, wet head, as the words scrolled before my hungry eyes. If I brushed against it, I knew I would come. Legs trembling, head light, I slipped back into the scene.

```
        I can feel your gaze heat the
tender places between my thighs. I know
you are contemplating what is yours,
waiting for me to swell, for the hint of
moisture to shine on the silky hairs.
You blow softly, your breath cool. I
twitch, catch my breath, moan quietly.
I raise my hips slightly, inviting
you. I want you to lick me. You kiss
the inside of my thigh instead, then
pull the tender skin with your teeth.
I push myself toward you, wanting you
to suck my tender inner lips, tug on
them gently until my cum flows onto
your tongue. You laugh knowingly and
run your tongue lightly over the very
edges of my lips, tormenting me.
```

Fingers pinched a hard nipple, a hand slowly drifted over a clit bulging with blood and heat, a low groan escaped as I found the rigid shaft and played it. Stroking fast, making my hips lift, but staying away from the one spot that once touched, I wouldn't be able to abandon. So good. Too good.

> My clit is throbbing now, exposed to you. Please, God--please lick it. I'm gasping, making small whimpering noises, wanting you to make me come so much. You slide one hand under my ass, lifting my hips toward your mouth, the other hand spreading the folds around my clit, making me jerk--your lips so near now. Please, baby, put your mouth on me. I need to come so much--suck me, please--The tip of your tongue pushes up under the swollen hood, pressing against the base of my clit--I cry out--oh, it's so good--

I read, reread, the words, my thumb at the base of my clitoris, on top of the hood, the length of my finger stroking from underneath, up the shaft and finally, finally, around the head. I needed a distraction, knowing I'd make myself come in another few seconds, and ever so briefly, I closed my eyes. But the words burned like an illuminated afterimage across the inner surface of my lids. Already far past the point of holding back. I read.

> Your lips take me then, sucking my clit into your mouth, circling it with your tongue. My legs are tight, the muscles in my pelvis contracting, the pressure building--ah, I'm getting close--

The ever-faster movement of fingers across a rigid clitoris, the erratic jerk of hips, the blurring of boundaries, the fusion of realities.

"I want to watch you finish. I want you to come for me."

Words typed on a screen, whispered in my ear, screamed across the silence.

I imagined watching, being watched. Everything blended, and I didn't know which one I was—reader, writer, voyeur. Everything was hard. Everything ached. And my fingers continued their relentless motion, clouding my mind.

In the end, I couldn't read. Couldn't see. All day I'd waited, and now it was so close. I wanted my clit to explode, needed to come.

```
     I'm moaning, moving against your
face, feeling my clit ready to explode-
-I need to come--oh, please, just a
little harder--oh, yes--that's it,--
I'm starting to come--oh, can you feel
me twitch in your mouth? Hips pumping,
coming now, so hard--sooo good--
```

With the orgasm still shuddering through my belly, with hands that shook so badly my fingers could barely find the keys, I started a new chapter.

```
     The ride home from work in rush-
hour traffic was a maddening combination
of pleasure and torture, and it had
nothing to do with the snarled, slow-
moving mass of vehicles.
```

CLINICAL TRIALS
PHASE ONE: CALIBRATIONS

Hunger is a powerful motivator. It's amazing the things
you'll do that you never would have conceived of if
you didn't need money to eat. Or in my case, to eat, pay the rent,
and put gas in the car. Not to mention next semester's tuition,
textbooks, and the occasional new pair of shoes. All right, it's
not quite that bad, but almost. I'm the typical struggling graduate
student, and fortunately, in a large university there are always
studies being done that pay volunteers to participate. Although
I've often thought that if you're being *paid,* you probably aren't a
volunteer, but something else. In terms of my newest assignment,
that "something else" turned out to be pretty hard to describe.

It started yesterday when I saw an ad in the campus newspaper
that said: **Study subjects needed for psychosexual
imprinting analysis. Must be 18 or older.
Please contact Van Adams at extension 6361 for
details**.

So I called, got the secretary in the experimental psych
department, and scheduled an appointment for this morning
at 10:15. When I arrived a little bit before the appointed time,
the same secretary directed me to an office down the hall. The
fluorescent lights in the cinderblock-walled, tile-floored hallway
seemed overly harsh as my footsteps echoed in the hollow silence.
The third door on the left was unmarked, but I knocked as I had
been instructed.

"Come in," a disembodied voice called.

The room was spare, and in the few seconds I had to scan it before my attention was drawn to the woman behind the functional metal desk, I didn't notice that any attempts had been made to personalize the space. University-issue bookshelves against one wall, filled with haphazardly stacked texts, file folders, and piles of papers; no rug on the floor; two worn, armless, upholstered chairs facing a desk that sat in front of what I presumed were windows behind closed horizontal blinds. The woman who glanced up with a remote smile appeared to fit the room. Late twenties, smooth pale skin, glossy dark hair pulled back from her makeup-free face, and big, dark, intelligent eyes. She wore a fitted linen blouse in a neutral shade, and although I couldn't see below the desk, I was willing to bet there were tailored trousers in a darker shade and expensive low-heeled shoes to match. Nice package in a professional, no-nonsense kind of way.

"Hello," she said in a silky, rich voice while standing to extend a hand. "I'm Dr. Vanessa Adams."

"Robbie Burns." I shook her hand, wondering how I appeared to Dr. Adams in my threadbare jeans, striped polo shirt, and sneakers. At least I'd had a haircut recently, so my collar-length chestnut waves looked fashionably shaggy as opposed to just plain old messy. At least my eyes, an unusual gray-green, were distinctive. And why that should matter, I hadn't a clue.

"You're here about 769, correct?" At my confused expression, she smiled absently. "Sorry. The multivariant sexual stimulus reaction study."

I held up the page from the campus rag where I had circled the small notice in red. "Would that be this?"

"That would be the one."

I thought I saw another trace of a smile, but I couldn't be certain. She settled down behind her desk and gestured me to one of the chairs that had probably once graced a student lounge but now should have adorned a trash pile somewhere. I sat and waited while she opened a folder and took out a number of forms. The first one she turned in my direction and pushed across the desk. "This is a nondisclosure statement. I'd like you to read it, ask any questions you might have, and sign it before I begin the intake interview."

"There's an interview?"

"Yes," she replied evenly. "There are certain screening criteria which are necessary for inclusion as well as exclusion from the study. The questions I will be asking are both personal and confidential—for you *and* for the study." She paused, studying *me*. "And before we go any further, I need to see proof of age, please."

I grinned and reached into my back pocket for my wallet. After opening it to the clear window that displayed my license, I passed it across the desk for her perusal. "Twenty-five."

"Thank you."

She passed the wallet back, and I replaced it automatically as I scanned the page before me. It was a standard nondisclosure form essentially saying that I couldn't tell anyone the details of the study, the questions I had been asked prior to engaging in the study, or the activities I might be involved in as a study participant. I signed it and handed it back. Dr. Adams took it, tucked it neatly away, and pulled out another page filled with blanks and boxes. Eventually we finished with my name and birth date and other vital statistics. The initial round of questions covered standard medical, family, and social history-type things. She dispensed with them quickly and moved on to the good stuff.

"The remaining questions will be personal ones relating to your sexual preferences, activity, and function. Is that acceptable?"

"Fire away."

"Are you single?"

"Yes."

"Heterosexual, homosexual, bisexual, or transgendered?"

"Lesbian." This was getting interesting. She didn't look up as she checked off boxes in various columns.

"Would you say that you have any kind of sexual dysfunction?"

I hesitated. "Does *not enough* count as a dysfunction?" I thought, but I couldn't be certain, that the corner of her mouth twitched.

She looked up and met my eyes, her face completely composed. "We're more interested in such things as anorgasmia, premature orgasm, or anything which you would define as a physical or psychological problem associated with sexual activity."

Anorgasmia. Thank God for those two years of Latin in high school. But didn't the absence of orgasm follow from my question regarding not enough? *Oh. Anorgasmia as in "the inability to have" orgasms.*

"No. Given the opportunity, I don't have any problem coming, and I generally have pretty good control." *Of course it's been so long, who can remember.*

"Good."

She made another little check mark.

"Do you masturbate?"

I bit the inside of my cheek to prevent one of those stupid responses such as "Is the pope Catholic?" and replied, "Yes."

"Frequency?"

"Yes. I mean...ah...three, maybe four times a week."

"You would be required to refrain from orgasm either with a partner or via masturbation for the duration of the study. Is that acceptable?"

"How long will the study last?" They were going to have to pay me a lot of money for this.

"I can't say how long your participation would be. It will really depend upon your response to the various stages. A week, possibly several."

"How will you know if I'm compliant?"

She still didn't smile, but her dark eyes twinkled. I was certain of it. "It's the honor system."

I grinned. "Agreed."

"Are you able to masturbate to orgasm while being observed?"

Her head was bent over the forms again, her pen raised above another little box. The study was getting more and more interesting by the second, and I was still only in the interview stage.

"Yes. Who's going to be observing?"

She raised her head. "I am."

I have no idea what showed in my face when my clit twitched. Hers revealed nothing.

"If you feel uncomfortable and prefer not to participate in the study," she said gently, "just say so, and we'll terminate."

"I'm okay so far." I took a breath and forced myself to relax. "Is there going to be group activity?"

"Only in the advanced stages of the study, and you may never get to that point." She leaned back in her chair and her voice took on a professorial tone. "The study is designed in levels, or tiers, and these strata are individualized depending upon the study subject's reactions to the test stimuli. Your responses to the early stages will determine the direction and nature of subsequent interactions. Although each set of study criteria is standard, not every subject will participate in the same sequence."

Somewhere out of that doctor-speak I think I got that what was going to happen would depend a lot upon how I performed in whatever it was we were going to be doing. I was curious, more than curious. Intrigued and not a little turned on. I'd always considered myself a sexual adventurer—at least I'd never said no without trying something. Okay then. Masters and Johnson, here I come.

"That sounds fine."

Another sheet of paper appeared. More blanks, columns, and boxes.

"Do you object to viewing sexually explicit images?"

"No."

"Do you find sexually explicit images arousing?"

"Sometimes."

"Do you use sexually explicit images as a tool during masturbation?"

Fortunately, I don't blush easily, and we were far beyond that point already anyway. "Sometimes."

"Literature, photographs, or videos?"

"All of the above."

Check. Check. Rustle. Rustle. I was getting wet. The interview couldn't have been more clinical. The subject, however, was getting to me. Talking about sex in any form, in any fashion, under almost any circumstance, turns me on.

"Have you ever used sexually explicit images during mutual masturbation with a partner?"

"How many people are going to read the interview form?"

Dark eyes met mine. "One. Me."

"Yes, I have."

Dr. Adams put down her pen and placed both hands on the desk, her fingers lightly clasped. She regarded me with a slight tilt of her head and a contemplative expression. "If at any time, for any reason, you want to withdraw from the study, you simply need to tell me. I will be administering all of the tests and collecting all of the data."

Well, that got me nice and hard. Administer away. The sooner the better. I nodded.

"I'd like to start tomorrow. Can you be here at 8:00 a.m.?"

"Yes."

"It's important that you be well rested and in as relaxed a state as possible. I know that may be difficult, but I assure you, there is nothing painful associated with any part of the study."

"I promise to go to bed early." I grinned.

"And please remember the stipulation regarding abstinence."

How did she know that the first thing I wanted to do as soon as I was alone was jerk off?

"Got it." After all, she wouldn't know. If I did it. Or if I just happened to be thinking about her when I did.

At five minutes to eight the next morning, I knocked on the door with the small plastic nameplate that read *V. Adams, PhD*. She answered immediately. Today, she wore a moss green shell, hemp-colored linen trousers, and low-heeled brown boots. Her lustrous hair was still severely tamed and tied back with a scarf.

"Good morning, Ms. Burns."

I laughed. "Could you call me Robbie? There's no way I'm going to be able to get excited if you keep calling me Ms. Burns."

"Get excited?" she asked as we started to walk down the hallway in the direction she indicated with a raised hand.

"Well, the only reason I can figure for the questions you asked yesterday and the stipulation that I not jerk...ah, have an orgasm any time except during the course of the study is that I'm going to need to do it here."

"Let's save this conversation for later," she replied evenly. She removed several keys from her pocket and opened an unmarked door at the end of a hallway. Inside was one large room that held a leather recliner in the center surrounded by electronic equipment on rolling carts, a bank of video monitors, and a small glassed-in booth in one corner. From what I could make out, the interior of the booth was wall-to-wall equipment. I also saw a microphone and headset resting on the counter.

Dr. Adams checked the thermostat just inside the door and turned it up. The room was already quite warm. Not overly so, but, I realized, warm enough that someone without much in the way of clothing would be comfortable. Holy shit.

"Today," she said as she gestured to the recliner, "we are just going to establish baseline values." She leaned down, opened a drawer in the bottom of the oversized chair, and withdrew two white sheets, one of which she spread out over the recliner. Turning to me, she held out the other. "Please undress completely and sit here. I have a few notes to make before we begin."

"I guess you'll tell me what I need to do when the time comes, huh?"

"Don't worry. You'll be given specific step-by-step instructions."

Under other circumstances, that sounded like it could be fun. The psychologist went into the tiny booth and must have adjusted the lights, because the overheads in the main room dimmed and the booth went completely dark. I knew she was in there, but I couldn't see her. It's not like I didn't know what was coming. Ha ha. I took off my clothes and got as comfortable as possible, which wasn't very. Hell, my clit was the only thing that *wasn't* twitching.

It couldn't have been more than five minutes before Dr. Adams came out of the booth.

"Ready?" Her voice was soft and warm. Or maybe it was just the room.

"All set." I think I sounded pretty confident. Usually, I *am* pretty confident about most everything, particularly sex. At the moment, I was terrified I might have performance anxiety and blow the very handsome stipend she'd mentioned the day before. Besides that, I wanted to appear studly in front of her. Since she hadn't given me the slightest reason to think she had any interest in me whatsoever other than as a study subject, I couldn't say why.

"Good. I'm going to be connecting you to various monitoring devices," she said as she rolled the carts containing the electronic equipment closer to me.

Most of what she attached I recognized—EEG pads on my forehead, EKG leads on my chest, arms, and legs, and a blood pressure cuff around my left biceps. When she motioned me to lean forward so she could run a thin flexible strap around my chest just below my breasts, I asked, "What's that for?"

"Respiratory rate and excursion."

She was so matter-of-fact about everything that I relaxed without even realizing it. Until she reached for the little alligator clamp with the thin red and blue wires trailing from the tiny jaws.

We're talking minuscule, maybe a half an inch long—too small to be a nipple clamp. I had an uneasy feeling about where that was going to go.

"Uh..."

"This morning," she said conversationally as she stood beside me with the tiny clamp dangling from her fingers, "we're going to take baseline measurements during unstimulated masturbation."

"Isn't that an oxymoron?" I couldn't take my eyes off the little tiny teeth along the edges of the little tiny clamp. "Where are you putting *that?*"

"First question first."

I swear to God I heard a hint of laughter in her voice.

"*Unstimulated* in the sense that we won't be using any visual aids. I'd simply like you to masturbate to orgasm unassisted by anything other than...well, whatever you ordinarily use in terms of mental encouragement."

"So fantasizing is okay?" I was struggling not to inch my way over to the far side of the chair. Escape was impossible at this point, unless I wanted to hotfoot it buck naked through the psychology building with electrodes hanging off my body.

"Absolutely. This," she said, indicating the device in her hand, "is a tonometer, designed to measure turgidity in the clitoris." She must have seen my pupils dilate. "I promise, you won't even know it's there."

"Where *exactly* are you attaching it?" There was no way she was closing those little tiny serrated jaws over the head of my clit. No fucking way. Not for a *million* bucks.

"Just distal to the junction of the corpora with the clitoral body."

"Translation?" I asked through gritted teeth.

"On the shaft at the base."

"Okay. Go ahead." As I was fairly sizable, I figured that thing couldn't hurt *too* much.

"I'd let you do it," she said evenly as she drew the sheet up to my waist and leaned over, "but it needs to be precisely positioned to pick up small variations in pressure."

I tried not to tense my thighs and told myself that this was just like a visit to the gynecologist's office as she spread me open slightly with the fingers of one hand and exposed my clitoris. Oh yeah, right. I never get a hard-on in the gynecologist's office. To my acute embarrassment, the second she touched me, I got stiff. Great. Then I felt the slightest bit of pressure in my clit, which only excited it more, and she was straightening up again and adjusting the sheet. I stole a look at her face, but she had that same dispassionate expression she always wore. I was just another lab rat.

"Comfortable?"

"Oh yeah. Perfectly." I was afraid to move in case something fell off. "There's a problem, though."

One of her perfectly sculpted brows rose infinitesimally. "Oh?"

"How am I supposed to masturbate with that little thing on my clitoris?"

"It may fall off, depending upon how vigorous you need to be. But all data is information. Try not to pay any attention to it."

Right. It should be a piece of cake to jerk off while attached to a bunch of machines with a beautiful woman watching and a little probe attached to my clit. No wonder they paid a lot of money for this.

"It would probably be helpful if you closed your eyes while I check the calibrations." Then she turned and walked away.

I leaned my head back and did as she said. Behind my closed lids, I could tell that the room got a little bit darker. I can't say that I was relaxed, but part of me was enjoying this. I'd liked her touching me, even in such a distant and clinical way. Her fingertips were soft and smooth and gentle as she'd attached the electrodes, and she'd handled my clitoris like she knew what she was doing. I pictured her eyes and the honeyed timbre of her voice, and my clit twitched.

"What are you thinking of?" her voice asked from a speaker somewhere nearby. The acoustics were good, and she sounded as if she were sitting right beside me.

Something told me that the only way this would work was if I was honest. "You."

"What about me?"

"That I liked it when you touched me."

"Would you touch yourself now, please."

"Is there a time limit?" I slid my hand under the sheet and rested my fingers on the inside of my right thigh.

"Not at all. Take as long as you need."

I kept my eyes closed as I tentatively ran my index finger between my labia and up to the undersurface of my clitoris. It was nice. It's pretty much impossible to touch an area with that many nerve endings and not feel something. Plus, my clitoris was intimately associated with my hand, and I had pretty strong conditioned responses to fondling it. Namely, I got wet after a few seconds, and if I fooled with it for much longer than that, I wouldn't be able to stop until I came. Out of habit, I carried those first droplets of thick moisture on the tip of my finger up to the head of my clitoris and circled it. I got a little harder. Intending to squeeze the head, I inadvertently brushed the alligator clamp with my thumb and caught my breath.

"Sorry."

"No problem. You're doing fine." There was a beat of silence where all I could hear was my own rapid breathing. Then she murmured, "I'd like you to tell me on a scale of one to ten how you would rate your current level of excitement. Ten being imminent orgasm."

God, she had a great voice. And a fabulous face. And she was watching me jerk off. The sudden realization that I was going to come in front of her, *for* her, hit me in the stomach like a sledgehammer. I soaked my hand.

"Robbie?" Her voice caressed me. "On a scale of one to ten?"

"Six." Christ, how did I know? I was hard as stone and wet and every time I ran my trembling fingers over my clitoris, my hips gave a little jump. Somewhere in my increasingly addled brain I wondered what that little device clamped around my clit was measuring now. Because I certainly felt like I was going to explode. I just needed something to get me past the last bit of nerves. "Can I use two hands?"

"Of course. Do whatever makes you feel good."

I slid my other hand between my legs and toyed with the swollen labia, manipulating my clitoris faster between thumb and index finger. I was starting to get that going-to-need-to-come-soon feeling. I picked up speed with my hand and moaned quietly.

"One to ten, Robbie."

"Eight," I gasped. I curled two fingers inside and rubbed my clit harder. "Oh fuck." I hadn't meant to say anything, but I couldn't help it. I pushed my hand deeper, working the head of my clit frantically with my fingers. My stomach gave a warning clench. "Jesus. *Nine.*"

"I know you're close," the soothing voice, so much like a touch, whispered from somewhere nearby, "but if you can, talk to me as you approach orgasm. Tell me what you feel."

I whimpered, I think. I turned my head and opened my eyes, trying to see her through the glass. I imagined her watching me, then I imagined her touching me, and the fingers stroking me rapidly to orgasm became hers. "I'm so hard now, need to come so much. Almost there...close...oh yeah. Just touch me right there...a little faster, baby. Just a little harder." I arched my back as the tendrils of orgasm fluttered and curled along my spine. Blinking, I tried to focus on where I knew she must be, but my vision was tunneling as every cell in my body ignited. "Oh God. Ten. Oh yeah, please, *ten.*" I surged upright in the chair as my stomach convulsed, my hand moving so rapidly as I forced out the orgasm that the clamp flew off my pulsating clitoris. "Jesus," I groaned, "I'm coming."

Somewhere in the middle of it all, the top of my head blew off. God only knows what the EEG must've shown. I fell back, boneless, my breasts heaving under the chest band, my heart hammering. It took me a minute, maybe more, to get my breath back. When I was finally able to open my eyes, she was standing beside me. Her face, that beautiful elegant face, was still and serene. But her eyes were liquid and hot.

I smiled, a lazy sated smile. "I screwed up."

"How?" Her question was curious, her voice throaty and low. She didn't move a muscle, but I felt her fingers on my skin.

"You can't use those readings for baseline values." I was still trembling and my voice was shaky. I sucked in air and tried to calm down. "That wasn't my normal self-induced orgasm." I shivered as an aftershock gripped me. "Oh man, not at all."

"Oh?"

I nodded, still unable to lift my head, watching her face. She was smiling now, too. "I shouldn't have thought about *you* while I was doing that. It turned the ten there at the end into a hundred."

Something close to pleasure flickered across her face and then disappeared behind her composed, clinical expression. But she couldn't hide the satisfaction in her voice.

"Well, I shouldn't worry too much about that. That's what bell curves are for."

And I couldn't wait to plot the next data point.

CLINICAL TRIALS
PHASE TWO: VIDEO

Do you think we could switch our sessions to the evening? When I come this hard, I'm not much good for anything for a while, and I have classes in the morning."

Two days later, the words still reverberated in Van Adams's mind, as did the memory of how Robbie had looked when she said this. She'd still had that soft, dreamy look in her eyes that she got immediately after she orgasmed. Over the previous three weeks, they'd had multiple sessions in the lab to establish baseline control values for the psychosexual imprinting study that Van was conducting in the experimental psychology department. By the time Robbie had made the request to change the meeting times, Van had come to recognize how Robbie looked throughout the various stages of arousal, at the moment of climax, and during the postorgasmic recovery stage. She knew how Robbie moved as she climbed through the levels of excitement to orgasm, the restless twitching of her limbs and progressively more frantic thrusting of her hips keeping time to the rapid movement of her hand beneath the crisp white sheet. She knew the way Robbie sounded, from the first slight hitch in her breathing to the soft moans and muttered pleas as she masturbated to orgasm.

Of course, Van's only interest during phase one of the study was in Robbie's physiological responses during the phases of sexual arousal and release as indicated by heart rate, blood pressure, brain wave pattern, respiratory rate, and pressure gradients in the erectile tissue in the clitoris. These readouts were carefully tabulated and charted, means and standard deviation calculated, and time-response graphs constructed. The fact that as Robbie approached orgasm she always turned her head to stare into the glass observation booth where Van sat watching, or murmured soft endearments while holding Van's eyes in the midst of her climax, or smiled up at Van as if they shared a secret while she relaxed in the aftermath of her release, had no bearing on the study and was therefore of no consequence. Besides, Van knew she was invisible inside the isolated chamber where she dispassionately observed, methodically recorded, and neutrally hypothesized.

I know she can't see me. Then why does it feel as if she is looking at me, for me? Why do I feel as if she's reaching out to me as she's coming? She's very beautiful when she orgasms—so expressive and free, unlike anyone else—

Van pulled herself up short, appalled by the way her concentration had wandered. Subjective observations such as these were of no clinical value. She was only interested in reproducible data. That's what the monitors and recording devices were for. After all, sexual arousal and orgasm were merely physiologic responses that could be explained and measured like any other natural phenomenon. Of course, there was a mind-body relationship, which was why the effect of various stimuli on response rates and magnitude were of scientific and behavioral interest. That was part of the purpose of the study. How a particular individual might appear during those brief moments of neuronal discharge and vasospasm had no bearing whatsoever on her work. And therefore did not warrant her consideration.

The alarm on her wristwatch sounded. 6:25 p.m. Robbie would arrive any minute. She was always on time. Of course, this was their first evening session, and perhaps she had been held up by something. A last-minute phone call, an engrossing dinner conversation, an afternoon interlude with a lover.

What are you thinking? She said she was single. Plus, she knows she can't engage in sexual activity outside the study because it might lead to orgasm. And she's not allowed to orgasm with anyone except me. Van gasped at the misstatement. *Except during the study. I meant she's not allowed to orgasm except during the study.*

Van slipped her fingers over the inside of her wrist and felt for her radial pulse. Sixty-eight beats per minute. Elevated. And she felt a little flushed.

Oh dear. I need to get to the gym more. I'm clearly out of shape. No wonder my stress-reduction biofeedback patterns are erratic.

She jumped as a knock sounded at the door, and her heart rate, low under any circumstances as a result of her daily two-hour workouts on the cardio circuits at the gym, skyrocketed to an unprecedented eighty beats per minute. She half stood as she called, "Come in."

The door swung open and Robbie Burns stepped in. Blond, blue-eyed, rangy and lean in low-cut Levi's and a navy blue rugby shirt, she looked confident and relaxed. Grinning, she said, "Hey. Reporting for duty."

"I didn't know you considered it work," Van riposted before she could stop herself. It wasn't her habit to engage in casual conversation with the study subjects. There was just something about Robbie that disrupted her usual modus operandi.

"Well," Robbie remarked, her grin spreading, "usually I don't consider coming a chore."

Van frowned. "You haven't given any indication that your performance during the study periods is significantly altered from your usual—"

Robbie laughed. "Hey, relax, Doc. I was just kidding. After the first time, when I was a little embarrassed just at the beginning, I've been *performing* pretty much the way I always do."

"I'm sorry. I didn't mean to put it that way."

Robbie tilted her head, observing Van curiously. "Is something wrong?"

"No, of course not." Van colored slightly, then looked down and hastily gathered her papers. "Shall we get started?"

"Sure. Can't wait."

As they walked down the hallway together toward the lab, their shoulders inadvertently touched. Van stepped hastily away, aware of a faint tingling in her arm. *Curious. She must have unusually strong galvanic skin conductivity.*

Robbie gave Van another inquiring look, but said nothing. Once inside the lab, Robbie automatically moved to the large reclining chair, stripped down, and settled beneath the white sheet. She watched as Van assembled the various monitors and began attaching electrodes.

"What's on the agenda for tonight?" Robbie asked as Van slid a hand beneath the sheet and applied the sticky pads across her chest, ending just below her breast. Her nipple came to attention as the edge of Van's hand brushed over it several times while arranging the leads.

"We're going to begin phase two with the addition of visual stimuli."

"Yeah?" Robbie tilted her head back to see Van's face. *I don't need anything beyond looking at you.*

Van found herself staring into deep blue eyes, mesmerized by the faint flickering of the dark pupils. She knew that involuntary constriction and dilation of the pupils occurred as an autonomic response to sexual arousal, and the small but powerful minicameras mounted in the ceiling had recorded that very same activity in Robbie's eyes in the seconds before and during orgasm. Van had expected to see that response in Robbie's eyes, but she hadn't expected to be so captivated by it. She'd replayed the tape after their first session a number of times to correlate the pupillary response to other biologic indicators, but she'd had to force herself to focus on the data and not on the mesmerizing expression in Robbie's eyes as she'd come. Even now, when that liquid gaze was merely holding hers, she felt an unusual stirring in her depths. *The thermostat must be set too high. It's very warm in here.*

"Dr. Adams?" Robbie asked softly.

"Yes?"

"Um..." Robbie looked down.

To her horror, Van realized that her hand still rested on Robbie's breast beneath the sheet. She snatched it away. "Just let me get the rest of these attached and we'll get started."

Robbie sat perfectly still while Van attached the EKG, EEG, blood pressure cuff, and thoracic strain gauges. She tensed as Van reached for the last monitoring device.

As Van drew the sheet up along Robbie's thighs toward her waist, she asked, "Is there something wrong?" As she had done during the previous sessions, she reached down to attach the small alligator clamp of the clitoral tonometer and found that her study subject was already in an advanced state of arousal. Robbie's clitoris was nearly fully erect and glistening with the evidence of considerable excitement. "This is a problem."

"Sorry," Robbie said with a small sigh. "I, uh..."

Straightening, Van kept her face expressionless, but her tone was involuntarily strident. "Did you orgasm before coming here?"

"No!"

"Sometime earlier today?"

"I wish," Robbie muttered.

"I'm sorry?" Van's tone was decidedly cool as she wondered exactly who had put her—*her*—study subject in this state.

"No, I didn't," Robbie said adamantly, wondering what the hell had gotten into Dr. Adams.

"I thought it was understood that you were to avoid situations that would lead to sexual arousal, and particularly pre-orgasmic turgidity, for the duration of study."

"Pre-orgasmic turgidity? Oh. You mean a hard-on."

"Regardless of the term," Van said acerbically, "you were to avoid such...circumstances."

"I *have* been—well, except during the night, when I can hardly help it." Robbie's voice rose in defense. "I told you at the interview that I'm used to getting off more than a couple times a week. I can hardly be held accountable if I have a damn wet dream."

Van's eyes narrowed. "That's another issue we are going to have to discuss later. For the moment, however, I'd like an explanation..." She caught herself starting to hyperventilate and ruthlessly lowered both her heart and respiratory rates with a series of biofeedback exercises, then continued, "For my notes. Since your baseline state of arousal is obviously elevated at the moment, I need to account for that in my data."

"You were touching my breast."

"Excuse me?"

"You were touching my breast, and it made me wet."

"That's all it took?" Van's voice was soft, surprised. *You're so hard. So wonderfully wet.* She forgot her biofeedback exercises and her heart rate shot up again. "I barely touched you."

Robbie's eyes found Van's again. A faint flush colored the psychologist's neck and the small triangle of skin left bare by her open collar. "That was enough."

"Is that...customary?" *Do you respond that way when other women touch you? How many women have elicited that response? How many have made you come?*

"No, it's not *customary*," Robbie replied irritably. *Even the sound of your voice is a goddamned turn-on.* She'd been looking forward to the session all day, and not just because she enjoyed the part where she got to get off with a beautiful woman watching. She liked the way Van would sometimes forget herself and look at her with a tender expression, and very rarely, with one of blatant desire. She knew Van was unaware of it, but it pleased her. She'd been primed for pleasure when she walked in that night, and for some reason, Van was in a bitchy mood. But it didn't change the fact that she was beautiful and sexy and she made Robbie hot. And the more Robbie looked at her, even with the heat of anger in her eyes, the hotter she got. Her clit jerked as if to remind her she had things to attend to. "And if you want to get that clamp on me before I'm a lot more than *turgid*, you'd better do it now."

Van held out the small clamp. Throat dry, her fingers trembling slightly, she said, "You'd better do it. I'm afraid if I touch you...it will only skew the data further."

"Oh yeah." Robbie drew a shaky breath and imagined those long, slender fingers closing around her clit. Stroking her. She got harder as her clit throbbed in time to her racing heart. "It'll skew something all right."

Van glanced at the EKG trace and frowned. "You haven't taken anything, have you?"

"What?" Robbie muttered as she held her clit, which jumped and jerked between her fingers, and closed the small clamp around the shaft at the widest part of the base. The pressure felt so good that her eyes closed involuntarily.

"Stimulants of any kind. Amphetamines?"

Robbie's eyes snapped open and she glared at the psychologist. "Fuck, no. Why?"

"Because your heart rate is very erratic and your respiratory rate—"

"I'm *excited*."

"We've established that, but these readings are indicative of a very high level of adrenergic—"

"I need to come," Robbie said softly. "Please...can we just do...whatever."

Van stared and struggled to collect herself. In what she hoped was a clinical tone, she asked, "What level?"

"Seven out of ten." The study required that Robbie rate her approach to orgasm on a scale of one to ten, with ten being imminent orgasm. Anything over five meant she was pretty well along and would be uncomfortable if she didn't eventually come.

"*Seven*," Van said in surprise. "How did that happen? We haven't even gotten baseline readings, and I still have to run the visual stimulation program. In addition—"

"It's you."

"What?" Van's words were barely a whisper.

"I...you...fuck. You make me hot." Robbie shifted restlessly. The insistent tug of blood and heat in her clit was making her a little nuts, and the device ruthlessly squeezing the *turgid* shaft did not help matters.

"Oh dear," Van murmured. "That's going to complicate things."

"*Things* are a lot more than complicated already," Robbie grumbled, stroking her inner thigh beneath the sheet with fingers that trembled. "I'm going to explode here. Can you just go take some readings or something so I can...take care of *things*."

Without a word, Van crossed the room, entered the booth, and dimmed the outer-room lights. As she turned dials and flipped switches, paper began to scroll and tracings flickered on small LCD screens.

"Before we begin," Van said in a detached voice as her eyes moved over the various readouts to ensure that everything was in order, "let me explain today's exercise. I'm going to show you a random video clip of a couple making love, which I would like you to watch through to the end without self-stimulation. If, however, at any time during the viewing of the video you feel the urgent need to masturbate, including to the point of orgasm, you may." She glanced through the glass. Robbie was only a few feet away on the other side and clearly visible in the soft cone of light from the recessed spot just above her chair. Her lids were heavy with arousal and the rapid rise and fall of her small, firm breasts beneath the sheet correlated with the level of stimulation indicated by Van's measurements. "Your present readings are all well above baseline. How do you feel?"

"Like I won't last two minutes," Robbie said with a small grin. "If you're going to show me porn, I'll probably come fast. I'm already so jazzed."

"Don't worry about that—just do your best. We'll work with the results we obtain," Van said dispassionately. "All data is information." She entered a series of numbers into the computer and watched as a randomly selected film segment appeared on her screen. The same segment would be displayed on a larger monitor where Robbie could see it. A young woman reclined on a floral sofa, a shaft of sunlight bathing her naked breasts. Another woman, also naked, rested between her spread thighs, kissing her exposed sex.

Robbie's readouts spiked, and Van felt an unanticipated wave of jealousy, which she immediately suppressed. *It's only a movie. She told you in the intake interview that videos excite her.* Still, she couldn't help but look up from her console and watch Robbie as the video played. Robbie's hands, outside the sheets now and resting on her thighs, moved restlessly in small circles as she watched the screen. Inside the booth, Van heard the rapid ping of the heart rate monitor. She glanced at the respiratory readout—elevated as well. The pressure readings from the clitoral tonometer were nearly at the maximum of any she had previously measured. *She's escalating quickly.*

"What's your level?" she asked through the microphone.

Robbie's eyes flicked from the screen to the booth. "Closing in on nine out of ten."

On the film, the reclining woman moaned and thrashed her head, obviously close to orgasm.

"Jesus," Robbie muttered. "I really want to come."

Van's stomach tightened as she continued to make notations on the graph sheet spread out in front of her. Robbie's voice was thick and heavy, and the sound of her desire was like honey in Van's veins. *Touch yourself. I want to hear you come.* Van bit her lip to hold back the words. In the background, the moans and cries from the video heightened in pitch and increased in volume. A flicker of movement in the other room caught Van's attention, and she saw Robbie's right hand slide beneath the sheet. She knew without looking that all the measurements had peaked. Some had even gone higher than any of her previous recordings. The sound of Robbie's heartbeat raged in the small space. *Do it. God, I know how badly you need to. Do it.*

The clitoral tonometer spiked again, higher this time, at the same time as Van heard Robbie's desperate whisper.

"I'm sorry. I can't wait."

Van watched, the monitors forgotten, as Robbie arched her back and groaned at the first touch of her fingers on her clitoris. On the small screen to Van's right, the woman climaxed with a sharp cry. Van felt a surge of wetness between her thighs. She kept her hands on the counter. Robbie moaned again, and Van's vision blurred.

Five minutes later the film had ended and the monitors screamed around her. Van looked at the readouts, all of them nearly off the chart, and still, Robbie had not achieved orgasm.

"Robbie," Van said quietly. "What is it?"

Robbie slumped in the chair, panting. "I can't do it. Fuck, I just can't get there."

Van's eyes flickered over the measurements. *Oh God, you poor baby.* "Do you want me to run another film?"

"No," Robbie gasped, straining to see into the dark booth. "Could you come out here for a minute? Please."

Concerned at the note of pain in Robbie's voice, Van hurried to her side. She stopped herself just as she extended a hand to touch her sweat-streaked face. "Robbie?"

"It's okay," Robbie murmured, her eyes riveted on Van's face as she began to stroke herself again. Within seconds, her hips lifted, her back arched, and she cried out sharply, shuddering into orgasm. When the tremors slowed, she regarded Van with a lazy grin. "I just needed the right picture."

Van trembled, her hands clenched at her sides, her senses reeling. *You can't know what a beautiful picture* you *make like this.*

"You okay, Doc?" Robbie inquired gently when Van said nothing.

"Just fine," Van finally replied, smiling inwardly. *Picture perfect.*

CLINICAL TRIALS
PHASE THREE: ASSIST MODE

D r. Vanessa Adams sat in the observation booth next to Dr. Gloria Early, her co-investigator in the sex-stim response study, taking notes on the progress of one of their advanced simulations. She barely registered the beeps, pings, and buzzes of the plethora of electronic equipment that surrounded her. Her attention was riveted on the study subject in the support module in the center of the lab. The recliner that had previously occupied that space had been replaced with a body-conforming platform sporting adjustable side panels that swung over the top once the subject was seated. The panels slotted together to form a partition between the subject's upper and lower body so that she could move comfortably from side to side, but she could not see or touch anything below her waist. A video monitor was suspended from the ceiling and displayed continuous images of erotic encounters. The subject had been provided with a remote control to stop, reverse, fast-forward, or replay any sequence she desired.

"Fifteen minutes of video viewing and the arousal index is still low," Early noted conversationally. "Just below five."

"We know she's a responder," Van replied. "Can you bring up the comparative tracings from the first run?"

Early opened a file and displayed the data on an adjacent screen. Van scanned it quickly.

"Baseline readings are essentially the same, but the escalation curve is much flatter this time. Acclimation effect," she suggested. "The subject appears to have a blunted response to the repetitive viewing of the same or even similar erotic images."

"Hmm. Somewhat analogous to acquired drug tolerance."

"Yes! Exactly." Van made a note. "We should compare the baseline values among subjects to the rapidity with which acclimation occurs—it may be that those with a lower threshold to visual excitement will maintain an accelerated effect, even upon restimulation." Her eyes shone with enthusiasm. "It's possible that we've been looking at the response curve in reverse—it may not be the *stimulus* which is significant, but the receptor sensitivity in the subjects themselves." In the midst of her theorizing, she envisioned Robbie stretching and smiling as she luxuriated in the afterglow of orgasm. Her *baseline arousal state is very high—higher than any of the others—and she has shown no blunting in the response curve with time. In fact, she seems to reach the critical threshold in an accelerating pattern. The last time—*

A series of beeps drew both investigators' attention back to the monitors.

"Ah, good. Level six," Early observed. She flicked the switch on an intercom near her elbow and buzzed the adjoining lab. "Sonja? Come in—she's ready." Then she keyed the mike to the experimental chamber and addressed the subject. "The assisted-mode phase is about to begin. You may continue to watch the video, fantasize, or employ any other maneuver to enhance the experience. You may also give instructions if there's something you need. All set?"

"Yes," the subject responded, her voice already heavy with desire. She indicated no uncertainty or nervousness, but kept her face turned toward the monitor and the continuous loop of sex. Her attention did not deviate even when a door on the opposite side of the room opened and closed quietly.

A short-haired brunette in a forest green blouse and trim, tan slacks moved quickly across the room on a path that kept her out of the line of vision of the study subject. She quickly knelt by the foot of the slightly elevated modular support in the deep vee that had been removed from the far end of the table. The subject's spread legs were comfortably supported on extensions on either side of the access area. Sonja placed her open hand on the subject's left inner thigh. The subject jerked infinitesimally, and her heart rate rose to 120 beats per minute.

From where she sat, Van could see both women. She didn't need to see the readouts on the recorders in the booth to know that the subject was substantially aroused. It was apparent in the combination of dreamy pleasure and anxious anticipation on her face. Van watched as Sonja began to run her fingers up and down the inside of the woman's thighs, stopping each time just as her fingertips brushed the swollen sex.

"Oh," the subject sighed. "That's nice."

"Level seven," Gloria Early commented quietly.

"Yes, expectancy escalating."

Van heard the subject moan, saw her hips clench and twist slightly, and watched on the close-up videocam as Sonja traced her fingertips over the glistening, slick folds. The subject gasped, her legs tensing. Heart rate 140.

"Steady progression," Van murmured, unable to look away from the subject's face. Over the microphone came the sound of increasingly rapid breathing and faint sporadic moans. "Level?"

"Eight."

Sonja leaned closer and blew warm air teasingly across the erect clitoris that she held exposed with her thumb and finger. The subject groaned, staring down the length of her body, unable to see the woman pleasuring her. "Oh God. That feels so good. Are you going to lick me? Oh, I want you to."

"Clitoral spike," Early stated. "Ninety percent of previously recorded maximum."

Van glanced at the close-up image on the monitor by her left hand just in time to see Sonja place a tender kiss on the tip of the reclining woman's clitoris. The soft wail that followed sent a shiver down Van's spine. She could imagine the tense clitoris and the exquisite softness of warm wet lips enclosing it. For an instant, she imagined herself with her lips circling Robbie's erection.

Oh God, no! I can't do this now.

Sonja eased the clitoris between her lips and gently, rhythmically sucked. The clitoral tonometer spiked again to maximum levels and maintained that pressure.

"She's pre-orgasmic," Early said clinically, marking a note on a scrolling piece of paper that showed sharp spikes and a steady line very near the top of the page.

As Van watched, the subject closed her eyes, arched her back, and opened and closed her fists with desperate intensity.

"Please, please. Oh, suck me harder, please. I'm going to come soon. Make me come now...make me come."

Early started a counter on the computer to record the time in hundredths of a second.

Van could almost feel the rigid clitoris swell against her tongue and taste the ripe promise of passion. She fought back a groan when Sonja delicately danced her fingertips over the moist swollen flesh of the woman's sex, dipping her fingers into her and then out as she licked and sucked.

The subject sobbed softly and thrashed her head back and forth. "Oh yes! Oh, I'm going to come...oh, it feels so good! Oh... I'm coming now..." Her pleas ended in a final desperate wail as her heart rate screamed into the 160s and the strain gauge clamped to her exploding clitoris flew off. The stimulation levels peaked and fluxed at max levels as Sonja gently licked and kissed the erratically pulsating clitoris throughout the subject's orgasm, not stopping until the woman in the study module lay quiet and utterly spent.

"Oh, that was so nice," the subject murmured thickly, her breathing finally evening out as her heart rate slowly returned to baseline. Her clitoris remained swollen but without the tonometer, Van could not judge the rate of her recovery.

"We'll have some data skews at the end here," Early remarked with moderate irritation. "We'll have to find a better way to attach the clitoral strain gauge."

Van couldn't take her eyes off the subject's face, having never seen anything as beautiful as a woman in the first seconds after orgasm. As she watched, Sonja placed one more delicate kiss on the tip of the woman's clitoris and then glided away.

"Do you feel that you could achieve orgasm again?" Early asked after keying the microphone. "We'll need to reattach the tonometer to run another sim."

The subject slowly turned her face towards the booth. "Not yet. I...oh God...it was really intense. I don't think I can go again for a while."

"Okay, no problem, then," Early said. "Take your time getting dressed, and we'll go over the details of your next session when you're ready to leave." She reached out and dimmed the lights in the outer room before turning to Van.

"What do you think? Time to run a parallel sequence with another subject?"

Van thought of Sonja or one of the other lab assistants expertly manipulating Robbie to orgasm. Her head ached.

"I might have a slight problem."

"You *can't* just fire me," Robbie protested as soon as she sat down in Van's small, cramped office. She'd been rehearsing her arguments for a week, ever since the morning that Van had contacted her to inform her that she would no longer be needed for the study. She'd been so stunned at the unexpected call and the surprisingly devastating news that she hadn't even asked why.

Van leaned back in her desk chair and placed her reading glasses carefully on a pile of reprints that she had been perusing without actually reading. "It isn't an issue of being fired. Your role in the study is simply over."

"Why? I know that the study is ongoing and that there are other sessions that I haven't participated in yet."

"We don't use each subject for every stage in the study," Van answered patiently with a small shake of her head. She was ridiculously pleased to see Robbie, even though she had been studiously avoiding all thought of her since their abrupt final phone call. At least she'd been *attempting* to avoid thinking of her. Even immersing herself in work didn't completely obliterate the heart-melting innocence of Robbie's smile or the terrible, wonderful memory of her arousal.

"Well, you *have* to let me back into the study. Because something's broken and it needs to get fixed."

Van's brows furrowed as she leaned forward. "What are you talking about?"

"I can't come anymore."

"What?"

Robbie leaned forward as well, and had the desk not been between them, she would have put her hands on Van. Somewhere. Anywhere. She was desperate to touch her. "I. Can't. Come."

"Have you tried?" Van colored. "Well, of course you have, or you wouldn't know that you couldn't." She took a breath, not truly wanting the answer to her next question. "Are you speaking of orgasm during an intimate encounter with a partner?"

"No." Robbie ground her teeth. "I'm talking about me, myself, and I. My *usual* partner. The one who never fails to give me exactly what I need in whatever time frame I happen to be in the mood for. A five-minute quickie for medicinal purposes. An hour of slow satisfaction with my favorite erotica collection."

"Ah," Van began delicately. "Sometimes, we can experience a temporary decline in libido or a transitory inability to achieve..."

"Nope. Not me. *Never.*" Robbie took a breath. "I know exactly what the problem is."

"What?" Van asked anxiously. She couldn't bear the idea that Robbie might have something seriously wrong.

"It's the study."

"The study?" Van paled. "That can't be the problem. The study does nothing more than record your responses to sexual situations or stimulation. It doesn't..."

"I'm imprinted."

"Imprinted," Van echoed as if she'd never heard the word before.

"Uh-huh. Imprinted. On you. I can't come without you."

Van's mouth opened to form a silent "Oh." After a moment, she swallowed painfully. "I don't think we've ever encountered that result before."

"Well," Robbie said matter-of-factly, "you can start writing the case report. Every time I start working myself up, things move along nicely, just like always. I almost get there. Almost. But when I turn my head and open my eyes for that final push, you're not there."

"I'll have to talk to my colleague." Van couldn't think. She was flattered, aghast, concerned, and terribly aroused. All she could see was Robbie turning toward her, searching with her eyes as her body quivered on the brink, and finding her, tumbling into ecstasy. The image was devastating. Devastatingly wonderful. "I'm not entirely certain how to reverse this phenomenon. I suppose we could try aversion therapy or behavioral modifica—"

"I've got a better idea," Robbie interrupted. "Let's go out on a date."

"So what did she say?" Robbie's best friend TJ asked.

"She said," Robbie replied, straightening on the bar stool and assuming a clipped, formal tone, "'I'm afraid that won't be possible due to our previous professional relationship.'" Robbie licked the salt from the back of her hand, downed the shot of Cuervo Gold, and sucked the lime with angry relish. "She's driving me nuts."

"What are you going to do?"

"I'm going to camp out on her goddamn doorste—"

"Uh, Robbie," TJ interrupted. "Didn't you say that she was about five-six with legs for days and a face like a Greek goddess?"

"Yeah. So?"

"Do Greek goddesses wear denim jeans and high-heeled boots?"

Robbie snorted. "Not the last time I looked." With her good humor trying to resurface, she swiveled at the bar and followed her friend's gaze. The blood drained from her head and pooled directly between her thighs. Van threaded her way determinedly through the crowd toward them.

Her hair was down...

It was wavy. Beautifully thick and glossy and Robbie wanted to get her hands into it immediately.

...wearing the aforementioned denim jeans...

They were skintight and faded in just the right places and Robbie wanted to get her out of them immediately.

...and looking at Robbie as if she were the only woman in the room.

Robbie's heart danced in her chest, her stomach flip-flopped, and her clitoris shot straight into high alert.

"Van?" To Robbie's horror, the word came out with a squeak of disbelief. *Oh cool, Burns. Way cool.*

"Hi, Robbie."

From beside them, a voice interjected, "Hi, I'm TJ. I was just leaving. Nice to meet you."

"Nice to meet you, too, TJ," Van said without taking her eyes from Robbie's. "See you again sometime."

"Yeah, right. Right," TJ muttered as she made herself scarce.

Softly Robbie asked, "What are you doing here?"

"Looking for you. I called your apartment and one of your flatmates said you were probably here."

"Yes, but what are you *doing* here?" Robbie's eyebrows drew together into a frown. "This isn't part of the study, is it?"

The corner of Van's mouth lifted. "And what if it is? I thought you wanted back into the study."

"That's because I was desperate."

"Oh, and now you're not?"

As they talked, Van moved closer until her hips lightly pressed between Robbie's thighs. Her right hand rested on Robbie's left leg just below her crotch. The little space between them shimmered with the heat of their bodies.

"No," Robbie murmured, tilting her pelvis forward until her fly snugged against Van's. "*Now* I'm downright dying."

"Well," Van allowed the weight of her body to rest against Robbie's while bringing her mouth close to Robbie's ear. "There *is* one part of the study we didn't get to."

"Whatever it is," Robbie replied as she circled her arm around Van's waist and pulled her tight into her crotch, "I'm in."

"We'll see." As she'd done that first day, Van whispered, "Follow me."

To Robbie's everlasting gratitude, Van's building was only a short block from the bar, and in five minutes they were climbing the stairs to the second-floor apartment. They'd said almost nothing on the brief, fast walk, but Van had reached down and boldly taken her hand. The shock of Van's skin against her palm had made Robbie gasp in surprise. Van had only looked at her and grinned.

"Come on. The bedroom is back here," Van murmured as she led the way through the apartment.

"Uh, what—"

"Don't worry." Van stopped and turned so abruptly that Robbie walked into her. When she did, Van put her arms around Robbie's neck and her lips on Robbie's mouth.

"Oh," Robbie groaned as she slid her tongue into Van's mouth. It was better than any fantasy, and she'd entertained more than a few lately with herself and Van in the starring roles. She would have been happy to stand rooted to that spot the entire night, stroking the inner surfaces of Van's lips, sucking the tip of her tongue, probing for the spots that made her arch and groan. The pressure in her belly was a constant distraction, but she was in no hurry to relieve it. Eventually, it was Van who drew away, gasping.

"We mustn't take this out of sequence. It will skew the data."

"There's some order to it?" Robbie sucked on Van's lower lip, then bit gently.

"Oh, yes," Van moaned. "A...definite progression. Mmm, you have wonderful lips."

Robbie's head nearly burst. She was so desperate for Van's touch that she wrapped her fingers around Van's forearm to guide her hand between her legs. As if sensing her intent, Van stepped away. Her eyes were glazed, her chest heaving.

"No. Not yet."

"Then when?" Robbie asked urgently. "God, I want you."

Van smiled knowingly. "Really. On a scale of one to ten..."

Robbie growled and took a step closer, reaching for Van's hips. "Seven."

Van backed away. "*Really.* Well. We should move on, then." With that, she turned and hurried into the bedroom. Robbie hesitated only a second and then bounded after her.

"Stand by the side of the bed, please," Van said in as even a tone as she could muster. All she wanted was to feel Robbie's mouth again and hear her deep soft sounds of pleasure. With hands that trembled, she caught the bottom of Robbie's T-shirt and lifted it off over her head. Her gaze fell to Robbie's chest and she moaned. "Beautiful."

"Touch me," Robbie pleaded, all semblance of pride gone. "I can't take any more."

Van nearly broke, but with her last remnant of control, merely reached out and unsnapped Robbie's jeans. As she pushed them down, she allowed herself the pleasure of trailing the backs of her hands over Robbie's thighs. "You forget, I know exactly how much you can take."

"You weren't touching me before." Robbie's nipples were hard, her hips thrusting into empty air as the passion beat through her depths. She managed to step free of her jeans, but her knees were threatening to give out. "Before I was only *imagining* it was you. I'm going to come standing here in a minute."

"On a scale of one to—"

"Oh God," Robbie moaned. "Nine. Please."

"Lie down on the bed," Van whispered, trembling. As Robbie did, Van began to undress. She watched Robbie's eyes, her face, the rise and fall of her breasts, knowing with certainty exactly what she was feeling. She knew every nuance of Robbie's arousal. When she inadvertently brushed her fingers over a bare nipple and it stiffened, Robbie moaned and smoothed the fingers of her right hand along the inside of her right thigh. Van recognized it as a move Robbie made involuntarily when she was highly aroused and needed to touch herself. Van smiled, stepped free of her slacks, and stretched out on the bed beside Robbie. She placed her hand in the center of Robbie's abdomen, circled over the tight muscles slowly, then gently brushed Robbie's hand away from her leg. "I can't let you touch yourself. You're already far too excited."

"You touch me, then," Robbie implored. "I'm dying."

Van caught Robbie's right wrist and guided her hand between her own thighs. Fighting back a moan at the first exquisite touch of Robbie's fingers on her skin, she murmured, "This is what we call...a parallel...simulation." Her hips lifted as Robbie's fingers dipped into the moisture between her thighs. She held Robbie's eyes, which were hazy and huge with arousal as she closed her fingers around Robbie's clitoris. "Follow me."

"Oh, Van, I won't last," Robbie gasped.

"You will." Van sighed and rested her forehead against Robbie's, welcoming the heat that flooded her thighs as she stroked Robbie and Robbie returned her caress. "Remember, I know you. Now, I want you to know me."

A minute passed, an hour, a lifetime as, eyes holding each other fast, they climbed past passion to the crest of wonder where pleasure transcended flesh. Shuddering, smiling tremulously, Van whispered, "Now, Robbie. Now."

As their hands blurred, Robbie pressed close, her vision filled with the image that never failed to carry her away. Van. So easy. So right. Only this time, Van was here with her, coming with her. Her eyes were liquid with pleasure, her face soft with surrender, her skin flushed with the first surge of release.

"Oh, Robbie, Robbie," Van breathed as she finally closed her eyes and slipped into orgasm.

"Ahh, yes," Robbie uttered as her bones melted and her muscles dissolved.

Finally surfacing, Robbie traced her fingers over Van's cheek and laughed quietly when Van caught her fingertip and sucked on it. "How many more stages of this particular experiment are there?"

"Didn't I mention that earlier?" Van sighed and stretched, a grin flickering on lips swollen with kisses. "This was just the pilot study." She snuggled against Robbie's chest, wrapping her arms and legs around her. "And you definitely meet the criteria for inclusion."

Robbie found the sheet with one hand and drew it over them while burying her face in Van's thick, soft hair. Closing her eyes, she murmured, "Well, Professor. Sign me up."

About the Author

Radclyffe is the author of numerous lesbian romances (*Safe Harbor, Innocent Hearts, Love's Melody Lost, Love's Tender Warriors, Tomorrow's Promise, Passion's Bright Fury, Love's Masquerade, shadowland,* and *Fated Love*), as well as two romance/intrigue series: the Honor series *(Above All, Honor* revised edition, *Honor Bound, Love & Honor,* and *Honor Guards*) and the Justice series (*Shield of Justice,* the prequel *A Matter of Trust, In Pursuit of Justice,* and *Justice in the Shadows)*, selections in *Infinite Pleasures: An Anthology of Lesbian Erotica,* edited by Stacia Seaman and Nann Dunne (2004) and in *Milk of Human Kindness,* an anthology of lesbian authors writing about mothers and daughters, edited by Lori L. Lake (2004).

A 2003/2004 recipient of the Alice B. award for her body of work as well as a member of the Golden Crown Literary Society, Pink Ink, and the Romance Writers of America, she lives with her partner, Lee, in Philadelphia, PA where she both writes and practices surgery full-time. She states, "I began reading lesbian fiction at the age of twelve when I found a copy of Ann Bannon's *Beebo Brinker.* Not long after, I began collecting every book with lesbian content I could find. The new titles come much faster now than they did in the decades when a new book or two every year felt like a gift, but I still treasure every single one. These works are our history and our legacy, and I am proud to contribute in some small way to those archives."

Her upcoming works include the next in the Provincetown Tales, *Distant Shores, Silent Thunder* (2005); the next in the Justice series, *Justice Served* (2005); and the next in the Honor series, *Honor Reclaimed* (2005).

Look for information about these works at www.radfic.com and www.boldstrokesbooks.com.